I KNOW A SECRET

OTHER BOOKS
BY THE SAME AUTHOR

Fiction

- PARNASSUS ON WHEELS
- THE HAUNTED BOOKSHOP
- KATHLEEN
- TALES FROM A ROLLTOP DESK
- WHERE THE BLUE BEGINS
- PANDORA LIFTS THE LID (*with Don Marquis*)
- PLEASED TO MEET YOU
- THE ARROW
- THUNDER ON THE LEFT

Essays

- SHANDYGAFF
- MINCE PIE
- PIPEFULS
- PLUM PUDDING
- TRAVELS IN PHILADELPHIA
- THE POWDER OF SYMPATHY
- INWARD HO!
- RELIGIO JOURNALISTICI
- THE ROMANY STAIN

Poetry

- SONGS FOR A LITTLE HOUSE
- THE ROCKING HORSE
- HIDE AND SEEK
- CHIMNEYSMOKE
- PARSONS' PLEASURE
- TRANSLATIONS FROM THE CHINESE

Plays

- ONE ACT PLAYS

JUNIOR HAD PUT UP A SIGN

I Know a Secret

BY
CHRISTOPHER MORLEY

Illustrated by
JEANETTE WARMUTH

Garden City, New York
DOUBLEDAY, PAGE & COMPANY
1927

 PRINTED IN THE UNITED STATES AT THE COUNTRY LIFE PRESS, GARDEN CITY, N. Y.

To
H. F. M.
and to
Christopher, Louise, Helen, and Blythe
not forgetting
the two young Cassidies
and the
four young Snyders

CONTENTS

ILLUSTRATIONS

I know a secret that the night imparts
When bedtime ends day's honors and disgraces
And masquerades all stormy little hearts
With such deceptively angelic faces!

You shan't forget your green and golden youth,
Lying some day so dim and far behind you:
So, mingling simple fancy, simple truth,
Here are these little fables, to remind you.

You won't forget. And in all joy and pain
Life offers, dear my urchins, when you're older,
How Daddy'd love to carry once again
You, and all your world, upon his shoulder!

I KNOW A SECRET

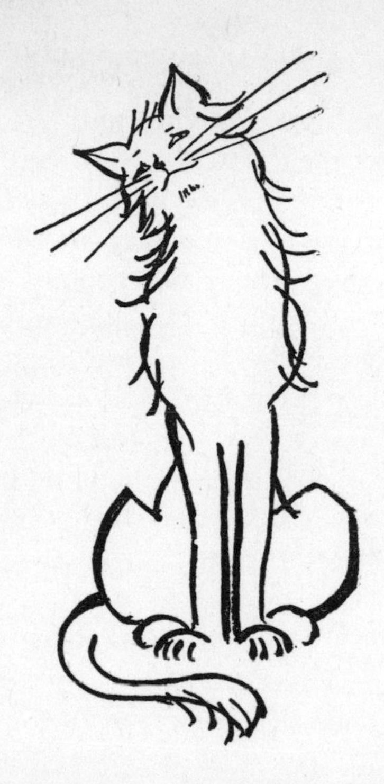

FOURCHETTE AND THE KITTENS

FOURCHETTE was a wise old cat who knew how pleasant it is to sit still and do nothing. The top of the cellar doorway was her favourite place. The doors had just enough slope to make them very comfortable for sprawling; the morning sunshine fell warmly there; and the kitchen was just overhead, so she could smell the cooking and get an idea of what the next meal was likely to be. There were many reasons why Fourchette liked the cellar door, though she was too lazy to tell you them all. It was raised above the ground so that she could keep an eye on the kittens, Hops and Malta, as they played about. Just below it, behind the laurel bushes, was an open window into the cellar. It was convenient to be able to flit in there if anything sudden happened. One jump from the sill to the washtubs, one more jump to the cellar floor, and there you were with all sorts of dark hiding places to choose. An experienced cat, no matter how comfortably you see her dozing, has always picked out in her mind which way she will run in an emergency. An *emergency* means something dangerous that happens very quickly, such as Fritz, the Snyders' dog, coming into the garden and making a dash at her.

Also, Fourchette liked the cellar door because the old weatherbeaten gray paint was just the same colour as her fur. She looked handsome lying there, and a cat of good family thinks of her appearance. Dogs, as you know, don't care. Donny, the long-haired sheepdog, will spend half the night barking through the woods after rabbits, plunge into the marshy edges of Gissing Pond, and come home with his coat full of burrs and mud. Does he mind? Not a bit. He chooses the softest place in one of the flowerbeds and lies down for a nap. But a cat can't sleep until she is clean.

This Sunday morning in summer everything was a little too thrilling for sleep. There had been kippered herring for breakfast, and an exciting fishy whiff still lingered in the bright air, mixed with the warm sweetness of the mint that grew by the back steps. When there was kippered herring, Perez, the Filipino cook, always gave the cats the juice from the can. The herrings had been lying in that juice ever since they were packed somewhere in Scotland; I have often heard Fourchette say there isn't anything more delicious. The only difficulty was that Donny was very fond of it too, and Fourchette always had to stand guard and hiss him away; while she was doing that the kittens, their pink tongues flashing busily, got most of the treat. Then they complained of being thirsty, but Fourchette had taught them to lick little drops of dew from the grassblades. This was more refreshing than the water in Donny's bowl, which had a queer taste because there was a big lump of yellow sulphur in it.

Few people know how many pleasant smells a cat's nose enjoys on a warm morning. That is why cats usually stay near the kitchen where the fragrance is more interesting. Some day when you are walking round the house you can make a list of the different things you smell. Fourchette, as she lay with her front paws tucked under her, could feel in her nose not only the breakfast herrings, but the first cracklings of the leg of lamb that Perez had in the oven for lunch, and the cool ashy whiff from the cellar entry below her, oily and leathery smells from the garage, ticklings of heliotrope and mignonette in the flowerbed, and a soft mixed sweetness that drifted out of the woods on the other side of the house. There was a cat-bird in the wood, who made a queer mewing sound as if on purpose to tease her. When Fourchette heard that her ears tingled and twitched just as they do when you blow in them.

There was the smell of the kittens. Kittens smell very fragrant, like warm sweet biscuits.

Louise knows that, and though she has been advised not to put stray cats up to her face, because they are often lively with fleas, yet I think I have seen her do it just to enjoy their smell.

And there were odours of dog. The smell of Donny, of course, was quite strong by the back steps; but Fourchette was used to that. Her nose also told her that Donny's friends Mike Hopkins and Fritz Snyder had been to call that morning.

Hops and Malta were squabbling over the Funny Paper. There was plenty of it for both of them, and by taking turns they ought to have been able to enjoy it without fuss. But they always *did* fuss about it and Fourchette had threatened many times, if that sort of thing went on, to burn it up, before anyone had seen it at all, in the big wire basket where rubbish is put. The *incinerator*, she called it, a word that had a great effect on the kittens. They knew that *sin* meant things that were unpleasant, and this long word *incinerator*, they supposed, had something to do with it. "If you do that, I'll put you in the incinerator," Hops once shouted at Malta when they were quarrelling over their croquet. Fourchette then explained to them that the word simply means something that turns other things into ashes. Fourchette, who was a well-educated cat, worried a good deal about the kittens' training. She was a Wonderful Mother, the kind handsomely described on the Greeting Cards, but there are moments when even they are less Wonderful. She felt, lying there in the sunshine, that she really ought to punish the kittens for squabbling, but she was in one of those drowsing moods that are so helpful in the lives of middle-aged cats. There are times when even kittens must be left to settle things for themselves, as we all have to do sooner or later. But the squalling went on, and a little angriness began to prickle in her lazy muscles. Her eyes opened and brightened, and she was just getting ready for a sudden spring when she was startled by a very polite voice beside her.

"Is there where Madame Fourchette lives?" it said, with a slight foreign accent.

Fourchette was greatly surprised; so much so that for a moment she forgot her dignity and her manners and simply stared. The stranger was a snail, a creature quite rare in Long Island gardens. A large, fat, and very comely snail with a round striped shell and two bright anxious eyes at the ends of queer elastic prongs. Snails are rather short-sighted, which sometimes makes their behaviour seem bold and forward without their intending it, for they are really quite bashful. So the visitor had come very close before he saw Fourchette at all. Now, when she gave a start of astonishment, the stranger retired nervously inside his shell. There was a long silence.

"I beg your pardon," said Fourchette presently, still a little bewildered. "Did you say anything?"

The snail, very carefully, put out one eye from under his shell and looked at her. His eye was courteous but wary. Fourchette almost laughed, he was really rather amusing, peering up like that.

"Forgive me for taking you by surprise," he said, "I am so short-sighted. I really ought to wear glasses, but with eyes like mine it would be so difficult to keep them on." This was true, for now that he had put his head out again his eyes were constantly moving forward and back and waving to and fro. He kept gazing at her with a sort of nervous hopefulness which Fourchette found slightly embarrassing.

"I introduce myself," he continued. "My name is Escargot, pronounced S-car-go—with a slight accent on the *go*. You see, I am French. And when I heard your name mentioned at the station, I thought perhaps I would have the pleasure of meeting another person from my own country."

"How do you do, Mussoor," said Fourchette. "I believe that some of my ancestors were French. But before my marriage I was a Roulston."

Of course Fourchette's notion about French ancestry was nonsense: her name was given her by Louise when the family had lately come back from Normandy. Her connections were all with the chain-stores: she herself had grown up at Roulston's grocery, down by the station, and her husband (when last heard of) worked for the A & P in Roslyn Heights. He was that rather handsome cat who used to lie in a sack of white beans in the window.

"That is a long journey, from France," she said kindly. "You must be tired."

"I am very glad to be here," he said. "I left France because, though it is a beautiful country, they have one very regrettable habit. They eat snails. I fled from my home to avoid being eaten. Perhaps *fled* is too hasty a word," he added thoughtfully. "At any rate, I departed. Tell me, Madame," he said, waving his eyes anxiously, "in this country, snails are not, I believe, considered a delicacy?"

"Certainly not," Fourchette reassured him.

"So I understood," he said, "from the conversation of an American family that was visiting France. I was one of a platter of snails that their cook, old Julie, a truly murderous woman, had gathered for their dinner. But when they heard about it, they refused to have those brave snails sacrificed for their nourishment. Julie was instructed to replace us in the garden. Our lives were saved, and I have come to America to express my gratitude. As you say, it is a long journey, but I affixed myself to the baggage of some travellers and got here at last. It is true that I had some difficulty in the Pennsylvania Station, where I just escaped being trodden upon."

He moved his eyes rather wildly, and Fourchette noticed that he did not look at all well. She hastened to bring him a fragrant leaf of mint, but he had retired into his shell, speechless. Escargot had fainted.

THE GRAPE ARBOR TEA ROOM

THE visitor lay quite ill for several days. They carried him tenderly to the rabbit hutch beside the garage, where he lay on a lettuce leaf. Rabbits are the most sympathetic nurses, and Binny and Bunny tended him with care, even trying not to keep munching when they were close to him because it made him nervous. Bunny, who is a white lady rabbit with beautiful ruby eyes, was as pretty as a Red Cross nurse in a white uniform. Fourchette had explained the situation to everyone, and they all tried to keep as quiet as possible. The breakdown was really caused by the fact that Escargot had tried to board his first Long Island train just at the time when the rush of commuters was at its thickest. Again and again the bewildered snail had approached the gate where he saw the sign OYSTER BAY. This had attracted him because he thought that people travelling on a line associated with oysters would be quiet and reposeful. But each time, as the gate was opened, the hurry of feet had frightened him away. This had gone on all Saturday afternoon and evening; it was not until early Sunday morning that he could get aboard a train. Even then he had to change at Jamaica, which was difficult. He had arrived at Roslyn in a very nervous state.

Mr. Mistletoe, the writer, looking out of his workroom window, was unfeeling enough to hope, secretly, that Escargot would be ill a long while. For children and animals all kept much quieter on the snail's account than they ever had for the sake of his work. By the rabbit hutch Junior had put up a sign which said

HOSPITAL!
DO NOT SCREAM
OR TALK LOUD

There were ten children and two dogs who did most of their playing just outside Mr. Mistletoe's window. Perhaps that was why Mr. Mistletoe, though only thirty-seven, had four gray hairs by one ear and two by the other. The four gray hairs were by his left ear, which was the one nearer the window as he sat at his writing. But now, out of consideration for the suffering snail, there was a good deal of silence. The four young Mistletoes, the four young Snyders, the two young Cassidies, rode their bicycles and velocipedes elsewhere. Donny, who is rather a noisy dog, turned his face away when the iceman or Masini the grocer or Craft the meat market came to the house. He pretended not to see, so he would not feel it his duty to bark. Donny is a sheep dog who has never seen a sheep. All his ancestors were trained to herd sheep, so naturally he has a strong family desire to do so too. But never having seen a sheep, he does not know just what it is that he misses. He thinks that tradesmen and callers are sheep and wants to herd *them*.

Louise and Helen and Blythe, the three younger Mistletoes, held a meeting at the Sand Club, a mysterious little summerhouse in the back garden, and elected Escargot an honorary member. Junior got out a special number of the *Roslyn Estates News*, a typewritten newspaper, to report the invalid's progress. Hops and Malta tried hard not to quarrel. Fourchette kept coming out from the kitchen with leaves of Mr. Masini's best lettuce or spinach to tempt the snail's appetite. Perez, whose bedroom in the garage was just beside the rabbit hutch, sat there in the evenings playing soft encouraging music on his ukulele. At last the invalid seemed to shake off his weakness. His eyes no longer peered timidly from under his shell, but came out and waved boldly and gratefully. He even disputed with Bunny her habit of eating the old sheet of lettuce when she made his bed fresh every morning. He began eating part of it himself. He was getting better.

The illness of Escargot had brought the neighbourhood together in a way nothing had done before. Every morning they would all gather round the rabbit hutch to inquire about the snail, and their interest in him seemed to make them forget any private feuds of their own. You would have been surprised to see them. Pigeons and chickens from Mr. Hopkins's, robins and squirrels from the woods near by, Fourchette and her kittens, Donny and Fritz, even Cap, the big red setter who hardly ever goes off Mr. Hopkins's grounds, all would sit quietly together beside the wire netting of the rabbit run while

Bunny made her morning report. Fourchette and Fritz, who were too confirmed enemies to be really friendly, could not pretend any pleasure in their meetings, but they ignored each other with careful politeness. If Fritz ever caught Fourchette's eye he looked quickly in another direction. Fourchette did not forget that Fritz had once killed one of her cousins, and Fritz remembered the scratch she had given him across the tenderest part of his nose. But for the time all were on their best behaviour. Even the chipmunks who live in the wall of Mr. Mistletoe's study, behind the bookshelves, ventured out to join the meetings. Mr. Mistletoe believes that these gay little chipmunks have a kind of night club in the passages between his walls and ceiling. Late at night he hears them dancing: they scamper and skirmish in there, scrambling and pattering to and fro. Light, light are their tiny feet, frolicking in the dry dusty tunnels between the beams. They frisk there like thoughts in the back of the mind. Mr. Mistletoe, as he lies on his couch at night, thinking severely of things he wants to write, has a horrid suspicion that perhaps sometimes they nibble at the electric wires. He wonders whether this could cause a short circuit somewhere, so that some evening he might start up and find the whole house wreathed in flame.

Day by day, as Escargot grew stronger, he delighted them all with his charming ways. His French accent was pleasant to listen to: it seemed to give new and quaint meaning to very simple sayings. His small face was humorous and polite; with shy courtesy he thanked them all for their kindness. Fourchette, who had reached the time of life where she meditated much on the meanings of things, perceived that Escargot was a philosopher. For as soon as he was tired, he withdrew into his spiral cell. What he did or thought about in there, no one knew, but inside that personal fortress he could not be interrupted. How lucky are people with shells, Fourchette thought.

Cats have a love of quiet, and this general truce that accompanied Escargot's illness was a great joy to Fourchette. A secret fear had been troubling her for some time. She had seen Mr. Mistletoe, a man of sudden tempers, looking rather fiercely from his workroom window while the animals were at their pranks. Fritz would bark at the rabbits, the kittens would scream at

Fritz, Donny would growl at them all or sprawl his heavy body in the flowerbeds, breaking down the irises and hollyhocks, squirrels would ride up and down the drive chattering on their velocipedes, and in the middle of all this hubbub Mr. Mistletoe would shout furiously from his window for a little silence.

"If this sort of thing goes on," he would yell, "I'll pack you all into the car and take you to the Bide-a-Wee." Fourchette had only a vague notion of what the Bide-a-Wee might be. But she knew, from whispered rumour among the cats and dogs of the neighbourhood, that it was a kind of farm, over on the South Shore, where animals were taken when they became a nuisance. It might be a very pleasant place, but animals have a strong sense of Home and hate to leave any place to which they are well accustomed. So the name became an omen, almost a Bad Word. The most embarrassing thing that one could say to another, in moments of temper, was "You go to Bide-a-Wee!"

So Fourchette's great idea came to her. The animals were all sitting around the rabbit run, and now that Escargot was getting stronger they were beginning again to be a bit noisy. One reason why animals squabble among themselves is that they are almost always hungry; and the sight of the rabbits, perpetually munching, was really irritating. It occurred to Fourchette that if she and Escargot started a tea room, in the grape arbor behind the garage, where the various creatures could always get something to eat whenever they wanted it, it would keep them all quiet and good humoured. Escargot, who was such a restful sort of person, would be an admirable manager for a tea room: and she herself could be waitress.

Bones, dog biscuits, milk, nuts, lettuce and carrot salads, corn for the chickens, a little oats now and then for the rabbits, fish occasionally for the kittens—Fourchette's eyes brightened when she thought of the car from the Roslyn Sea Food Market driving up the hill.

"But how would we pay for the food?" said Donny. "We haven't any of us any money."

"We'll arrange a course of lectures in connection with the tea room," said Fourchette. Just as Donny was a sheep dog who had never seen a sheep, so was Fourchette a well-educated female who had never been to lectures, and there was a vacancy in her life. She knew that whenever Mr.

Mistletoe was very hard up he went off somewhere and gave a lecture.

"Here we have Mussoor Escargot, a distinguished foreigner," she said. "People will always pay more for lecturers from abroad. He can give a series of talks."

"I don't think I should be very good at lecturing," said Escargot. "Why don't we all tell stories?"

The animals pricked up their ears at this. For all animals love stories. They get them not out of books but out of the exciting things that actually happen.

"A very good idea," said Donny. "You say the kittens need some education, that's the best way to give it to them. If you'll supply the food, we'll tell Hops and Malta some fairy tales that will put sense into them. They can't ever be more than cats, but at least they'll be cats with some respect for intelligence."

And the chickens, squirrels, birds, rabbits, dogs, frogs, spiders, insects, all the creatures of the Roslyn Estates who were sitting by the rabbit run listening, echoed Donny's idea. So the Grape Arbor Tea Room and Storytelling School was founded.

Now I must tell you just a word about the grape arbor. It was not much of an arbor, only a place behind the garage where a long grape vine trailed down from a tree beyond the fence, and was propped on poles. But the animals all liked that little back-lot because a few years before it had been a regular small jungle of briars and thickets, snakes and poison ivy and violets. So it still had something of the good smell and feeling of a wild place. You go to it by a little path that passes under an arch of lilac and round the end of the garage. Behind the garage is a strip of blue gravel. The wide branches of an oak tree overhang the fence, and it is all quite snug and private. By the grape arbor is the little workroom, built against the end of the garage, where you can go if it rains. The grass is coarse and ragged, but there is a hollow in the ground where the sunshine is very warm and yellow. You feel that you are by yourself, and like it.

So they hurried to sweep and clean the arbor. Perez, always good natured, was glad to help. Fourchette, in a clean apron, made the tea on an oil stove in the workroom, and served meals on paper plates on the ground. Escargot, sitting on a large grape leaf where he would not get walked on, was master of ceremonies. Junior painted a sign for the arbor and typed the menu cards. The news soon went round among all the animals. People got the habit of dropping in about the hungry time of the afternoon. It was understood that the stories told after tea were specially for the benefit of the kittens, but there were amusements for others too. Sometimes Perez, sitting on a little bench under the trees, would play music for the company, or the squirrels would give a climbing exhibition. Once the Gissing Pond Choir, the best singers among all the frogs of the neighbourhood, came up to give a concert. Escargot made a rule that anyone who caused disturbance or argument would not be admitted again. It was a happy time.

Mr. Mistletoe became curious about this congregation of animals behind the garage. He used to see them quietly slipping toward the back lot. He would hear the silken whirr of pigeons' wings as they flew over from Mr. Hopkins's barn, or notice a file of frogs and wild rabbits hopping briskly up the drive. Writers are inquisitive, and many times he went out into the garage and hung about in the hope of hearing what went on. But animals are shy and whenever he was near they pretended they were doing something else. The tales they told would never have got into this book if it had not been for Escargot. How that happened you will learn later. Meanwhile, here are some of the stories.

MR. LIVERWURST'S PICNIC

THE kittens were always delighted when the picnic season began. It was a family that believed in picnics, and from April to October one might expect, almost any fine day, to see Fourchette burst out of the kitchen door, sniff the air, and suddenly exclaim "I'm sickantired of ordering meals! Let's shut up the house and go for a picnic!"

Then there was hurrying to collect bathing suits, towels, sweaters, sun hats, water wings, tin spades, toy boats, pieces of string, the old steamer rug, paper drinking cups, all the odds and ends that fill up the car and make a picnic a success.

But no food. It was understood that a picnic was to relieve Fourchette of the strain of housekeeping. When she went on a picnic she didn't even want to know what she was going to have to eat. That was to be a surprise.

There are all sorts of places to go picnicking, depending on the weather. You can go out the Parkway, where you see the airplanes over the flying fields and have a fine view across those wide grassy plains. Later on you get into the pine woods, or even go as far as Lake Ronkonkoma—a name the kittens found it hard to say. Or you can go to Lloyds Neck, a wonderful region they highly approved. If you knew the lanes and trails of Lloyds Neck you could find your way past that huge oak tree (the biggest on Long Island) to Target Rock. Donny used to remark, a little anxiously, as he drove the car, that all those wonderful lonely beaches on Lloyds Neck were "Private Property." But in those days the Neck was very quiet, they disturbed no one and were never moved off. Indeed the kittens came to believe that the words *Private Property* simply meant a fine place for a picnic.

Or there was the lighthouse at Eatons Neck, another excellent shore to visit. Donny really preferred that. Though it was farther to go, it belonged to the government, and he felt he had a right to use it. Once when the lighthouse keeper seemed a little doubtful Donny produced his license. It said: *State of New York, Dog License Number 184525. Fee $2.25. Town of North Hempstead, County of Nassau. Dog's Name,* DONNY. *Breed,* ENGLISH SHEEP. Donny asserted that this proved him to be a tax-paying citizen, with a right to enjoy government property. The lighthouse keeper was so surprised at Donny's firmness that he let them go through and down to the beach.

But perhaps best of all were the picnics to the little Boat Club at Glen Cove. Because there, in case of a storm, you had the clubhouse to take shelter in. You were, so to speak, on your own ground and couldn't be turned off; and there was the catboat *Platitude.*

Hops and Malta, unlike most kittens, were very fond of the water. Even Fourchette, though she did not care much for sailing, admitted that a catboat was the most suitable kind of craft. A *platitude* simply means something flat and shallow, and she was. She had a centreboard, and was almost as broad as long. Donny used to say

that she had submarine l
strong breeze she had a ter
down into the water as
under. But on calm days, v
breeze, Fourchette sat in
verandah of the clubhous
kittens drifted about in th
wore their little green bat
old tire tubes, blown up
their waists in case of acc
calmed the kittens put t
board and hoped for a b
anything, but they alw
eagerly over the stern
floats. Donny, who was
fish, smoked his pipe an
looked quite like an old
if the wind failed altoge
and paddled the boat ba
kittens were always exci
twirls of silver bubbles
oar in the still water.
quietly relieved when th
dock. In her own tho
about water and once
too much of it about l

had run this delicatessen store for a long time. All summer, every fine day, he was busy slicing sandwiches and making up bags of lunch for people who were going on picnics. On Saturdays and Sundays he must have cut hundreds of sandwiches. But he never had a chance to go on a holiday himself. Indeed he hardly knew just what a picnic was. He thought about this a great deal, until he got quite savage. If you think of a thing for a long time and do nothing about it you get yourself in a rather queer state. So it was with Mr. Liverwurst.

One fine day Donny came in grinning cheerfully and saying as usual, "What a grand day for a picnic." He began giving his regular order for liverwurst sandwiches and all the rest of it. Mr. Liverwurst flushed red and began playing with his long sharp knife. Donny did not notice, he was busy looking in the glass case to decide what kind of cheese to take. He always found it a bit difficult to talk while ordering the lunch, because the sight of all the meats filled his mouth with wetness. But he swallowed several times, and then said firmly, "And please don't put any mustard on the sandwiches."

This was more than Mr. Liverwurst could

stand. Because he enjoyed putting mustard on the sandwiches, it was the only thing that made cutting sandwiches any fun for him. He lost his temper entirely. He thought of reaching over and spreading mustard on Donny's large moist black nose.

"I'll mustard you," he shouted. And then he suddenly ran round from behind the counter and threatened Donny very fiercely with the knife.

"See here!" he said. "Today *you're* going to stay here and run the store and cut up sandwiches. *I'm* going on a picnic instead."

Donny was greatly surprised, but Mr. Liverwurst's knife looked so dangerous he did not argue about it. Besides, all the different things in the glass case smelled delicious and he had often thought what fun it must be to weigh things on the scales and put pickles and potato salad in the little cardboard trays. So he agreed, on condition that Mr. Liverwurst would supply the lunch free. Mr. Liverwurst, sorry to have lost his temper, agreed to that. They explained politely to Fourchette the change of plan. Donny put on Mr. Liverwurst's white apron, and after making sure that the delicatessen man understood how to drive Dame Quickly, he waved them good-bye. Off they went along the Jericho Pike.

Mr. Liverwurst was in excellent spirits at first. This was his only holiday in ten years, he said, and he was anxious to learn what happened on picnics. But little by little things became difficult. Mr. Liverwurst, after all these years of delicatessen, smelt so strongly of meat and sausage and smoked fish that the kittens became riotous. Even Fourchette had to lean far over to the other end of the seat to control herself, and kept bursting into purrs of excitement. The kittens were leaning over from the back seat and smelling Mr. Liverwurst's coat collar, which made him nervous. When Hops, growing wild, jumped on his shoulder and began nibbling his ear the car almost crashed into a tree. As they went through Sea Cliff thc traffic policeman reproached the delicatessen man severely for careless driving. But it was not really Mr. Liverwust's fault, for by this time all three cats were almost sitting in his lap, and pricking their claws into his knees with playful good humour.

The kittens were so hungry that when they got to the club they had to have lunch at once.

It was eaten on the beach, so as not to disturb other members who were sitting quietly on the porch. Even so there was some scandal caused in the club by the way Fourchette and the kittens snuggled all over Mr. Liverwurst as he sat on the sand. There were complaints made to the Membership Committee.

Mr. Liverwurst did not eat much lunch. So much of his life was spent among food that he was glad not to think about it for a while. The heat on the beach bothered him, for in his shop in Mineola, among iceboxes and electric fans, it was always cool. Also three active cats climbing up his back and rubbing against his fragrant trousers made him feel hotter still. But Fourchette and the kittens ate enormously. Then Fourchette, growing a little ashamed of the way she had behaved, became very stern with Hops and Malta. They were soon in tears. They had to be consoled by the story of the Paper Bag Tree that is always told at picnics. It is a story about a family that always left a mess behind them after a picnic. They scattered bread crusts and bits of paper and banana skins and empty bottles in the woods. Then one morning they woke up and found that a Paper Bag Tree had grown in their yard. A Paper Bag Tree is a great untidy straggly bush that has little paper bags blossoming on every branch. From a distance it looks picturesque, but when you get near you find that in each of the paper bags is an empty peanut shell, scraps of silver foil, orange peel, and the top of a ginger ale bottle. When you see a Paper Bag Tree growing in anyone's yard you know that those people are not at all congenial.

After lunch it was high tide. Hops and Malta insisted on going out in the boat. Fourchette, uncertain of Mr. Liverwurst's ability as a sailor, thought it best to go with them. Mr. Liverwurst put on Donny's bathing suit, in which he looked so odd that Fourchette feared the smarter members of the club were laughing at them. After some confusion they got into the club dinghy and rowed out to the *Platitude's* mooring. Fourchette had a feeling of coming disaster, but now it was too late to turn back. They got the sail up at last, but very untidily. They had started off and thought that all was well, but then they heard shouts from the dock. They were towing the club dinghy with them, instead of returning it to the

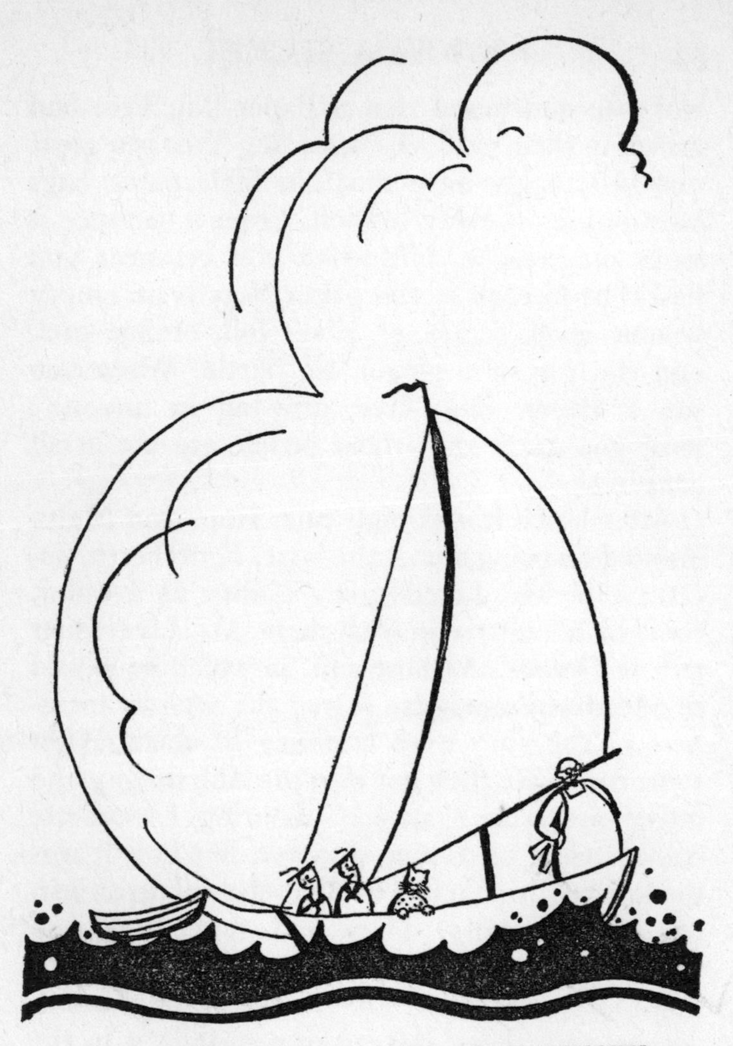

THEY WERE TOWING THE CLUB DINGHY

pier as they were supposed to. Mr. Liverwurst tried to sail back, but they had forgotten to put down the centreboard and the *Platitude* went mostly sideways. Also he did not really know how to make a landing, which always needs some skill. He banged into the swimming-float on the windward side, almost hitting some of the bathers. The boat was jammed there by the breeze. Trying to push off, the wind got into the wrong side of the sail, the boom swung over and knocked both him and Fourchette into the water. The kittens, wild with excitement, swarmed up the mast and would not come down. They clung to the gaff, yowling. Fourchette was politely pulled out by the Commodore of the club himself, which was a great honour; but her pretty foulard dress was spoiled, and she was in a horrible temper.

They drove back in a very peevish state. Fourchette was extremely angry with Donny when they got to Mineola. Donny answered her crossly, for slicing meat all day had made him rather fierce too. And the adventure cured poor Mr. Liverwurst of any desire to go on picnics. If you go into his store and say anything about picnics he will laugh heartily and say he is happier at home with his carving knife.

Fourchette laughed too, but not till she got home and the kittens were safely in bed. To this day her eyes grow a little wild when she thinks of the smell of Mr. Liverwurst's coat.

THE SCHEMING KITTEN

THERE was once a kitten called Pushkin, who was always full of schemes. He was so busy trying to plan things beforehand that you would have said he was not a kitten at all, only a very small cat. He tried to arrange everything so it would happen comfortably and nicely for himself. If a game of croquet was to be played, he managed always to be first at the box where the mallets were kept, so he could get the one with the pink stripe.

If the family were going down to the post office to get the mail, he took care to sit nearest the door of the car, so he could be the one to hop out and open the letter-box. The box was opened by twirling little knobs, like a tiny safe. It was fun to turn them to the right positions and hear them click, then swing back the glass door and take out the letters. Sometimes in the box was a yellow card that said CALL FOR PACKAGE TOO LARGE FOR BOX. Then he purred, because this often meant a surprise, a present of some sort from a grandmother or an aunt. He stood on tiptoe below the window and mewed gaily until Mrs. Breen came to see who it was. She could only see his ears and the pink tip of his nose, so she lifted the railing and looked out.

"Oh, hullo Pushkin," she said, "I thought I recognized your mew. Is everybody well at your house? Yes, there's a package. Please jump up here on the shelf and sign for it."

The other kittens would have enjoyed doing all this too, but somehow it was always Pushkin who had planned it beforehand and was the first one out of the car. It was like that with almost everything that happened. Pushkin had thought out what was coming and had made his own plans. I am not saying this is a bad thing. Perhaps it is wise. But I think he carried it too far. Sometimes he almost believed he was the only kitten in the world. He never thought that there had been millions of kittens before, and would still be millions of kittens hereafter.

In his usual habit of studying what was going on and deciding how it could be arranged to his own advantage, Pushkin had noticed a can of herrings on top of the icebox. That meant there would be herrings for breakfast tomorrow, and all afternoon he had that on his mind. One can of herrings is not very much among several hungry cats, and those who got down to table first would probably get the fattest share. So the question was, how to plan things so that he would be there a little ahead of the others.

There was one thing they were very strict about in that family, and that was the cleaning of teeth. In the bathroom each kitten had its own mug and toothbrush, and so that they could not forget, their father had drawn a picture of a very healthy-looking cat brushing its teeth. This picture was on the wall, and below it was written

DO NOT FORGET TO BRUSH YOUR TEETH
BEFORE, BEHIND, AND UNDERNEATH.

Sometimes, when their father and mother went to the bathroom to clean their own teeth, they would even feel the kittens' brushes to make sure they had been used. If the brushes did not feel damp, the kittens were sent upstairs again right away, to do the job properly.

Pushkin's idea, which he did not mention to anyone, was that if he cleaned his teeth specially well that night he could go without brushing them in the morning. Then he would get down to breakfast a little before the others and have first go at the herring. So when he went to bed he gave his mouth an extra good scrub. On the bathroom shelf there was a tube different from the usual toothpaste. Always full of ideas about things, Pushkin decided that this must be some specially good toothpaste reserved for his parents. So he used it liberally. It did not taste quite like the paste he was accustomed to, but it made his teeth very white and he went to bed quite contented. He snuggled down under the covers, purred to himself a little while, and then he was asleep. He rested soundly and dreamed about fish.

Now it was morning, one of those bright mornings when everything feels perfect and your legs are full of running. Rhododendrons were in flower under the dining-room windows, the trees were chirruping with bird-song, and all round the house was the beautiful smell of cooked herrings and a noise of purrs. The father and the mother cat sat at the ends of the table, and already the other kittens were guzzling their share, but there was no sign of Pushkin. Then a queer moaning sound was heard on the stairs, and he rushed into the room. He was a sight. His eyes were wild and green, his fur stood on end, his tail was puffed up with fright. He could not seem to speak, only utter a dreadful yowling, He rushed madly round and round the table until they thought he must have a fit. For that does happen to kittens sometimes, when they first discover how very exciting it is to be alive.

But there was something so desperate in Pushkin's behaviour that they knew it was serious. His mother sprang from her chair and rushed after him. Three times she chased him round the table, until the other kittens were tempted to join the wild pursuit. But the herrings were too good, and they stayed where they were. His mother seized him at last and looked at him.

"Good gracious!" she exclaimed. "His teeth are clenched tight together! He can't open his mouth, he must have lock jaw. Telephone for Dr. Jessup!"

But his father, examining closely, saw a kind of hard white glue that was sticking Pushkin's teeth together. The scheming kitten had cleaned his teeth with a tube of very strong cement that had been left in the bathroom when his father mended a broken soap-dish. They got his mouth open presently, with hot water and a screw-driver, but by that time the other kittens had finished the herrings. They tried not to purr while they ate, but they could not help it. Push-kin, his sharp teeth stuck fast, sat watching them and his eyes were full of angry tears.

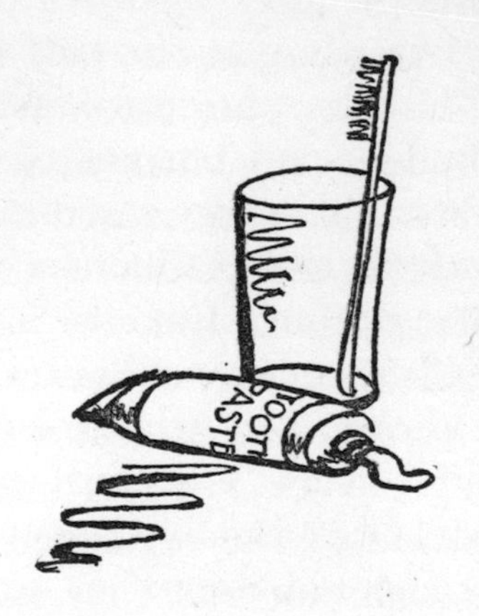

THE BIRDHOUSE OF LINCOLN LOGS

LIKE all small boys, Christopher was a great student of the advertisements in magazines. Especially the advertisements that offered souvenirs, premiums, free samples of anything. All sorts of queer surprises turned up in the crowded letter-box at the post office—little packages of biscuits and breakfast foods and toothpaste, badges and buttons of every kind, catalogues, First Aid outfits, instruction booklets on How To Play the Harmonica or How To Carve a Bullfrog From a Cake of Soap.

Although Christopher's allowance was only fifteen cents a week, Mr. Mistletoe observed enviously that his son always seemed to have plenty of ready cash. Occasionally, however, Christopher had a sudden impulse to put it all into a toy bank from which it could not be got out. Then Mr. Mistletoe had to make an advance to pay for the box of crayons or ice cream cone that seemed very urgent just at that moment.

But one of the advertisements that caught Christopher's fancy resulted in a real story. It was an advertisement about a birdhouse made of "Lincoln logs." It was a charming idea: a little birdhouse made of rough strips of wood with the bark still on, so that it looked like a tiny log cabin—in fact, it was planned to look like the famous log cabin where Abraham Lincoln was born. Christopher sent along the money and the birdhouse arrived. It came in pieces, with instructions, and he and Mr. Mistletoe enjoyed fitting it together. It was put up in a tall tree in the back lot.

The houses that people live in have a great influence on their thoughts and behaviour. The blackbird who came to live in that cabin was evidently a queer fellow by nature, but when he settled there he became the talk of the neighbourhood. I think he imagined that because he lived in that log cabin he was a kind of Abe Lincoln among birds. Certainly he looked the part, for he was unusually tall and shambling, with long shanky legs and rusty black plumage. It was even said that when he went out searching for worms he wore a little plug hat and carried an umbrella and an old-fashioned satchel. He put up a scrap of shingle on his cabin that said LAW OFFICE, and earned a modest living by settling disputes among the birds. Birds have a great many problems, for they are quick-tempered and their life is complicated. Building a nest, for instance, involves the question of who owns the material of which the nest is built; and then some other bird may lay claim to a special location on a convenient branch. Because your parents nested in a certain crotch have you a right to nest there too the following year? Then also, these problems of bird life mostly concern the mother birds, and ladies are always sensitive about property.

Sometimes a lively scolding and chattering would be heard in the green apartments of the trees. A feather or two would come floating down. Then there was a flutter and angry birds came flying to the log cabin. They perched on a limb and screamed their quarrel to the lawyer while he appeared at his door and listened patiently. He tried to get them to talk one at a time; he never decided anything without calling in witnesses and hearing both sides. He gave judgement in some very important cases which became famous in those days. There was the case *Fourchette vs. Catbird.* Fourchette brought suit against Catbird because Fourchette had been shut up in the cellar for mewing under Mr. Mistletoe's window while he was working. But it was not Fourchette at all, it was the catbird. Fourchette said that Catbird had done this out of deliberate malice, on purpose to get her into trouble, Another interesting case was that of *Chickens vs. Pigeons.* Mr. Hopkins's hens wanted to restrain the pigeons from coming inside the henyard to pick up grain that was scattered there for the chickens. The pigeons maintained that some of that grain had been intended for them, but had been carried inside the netting by a strong wind. Lawyer Blackbird was able to show, by referring to the Weather Bureau, that there had been no wind at all that day. The chickens won their case.

So Blackbird became quite well known among birds interested in the law. More than once birds from the Mineola Courthouse flew over to the Roslyn Estates to consult him.

But his own clients were not always grateful.

Sometimes, when the dispute was settled, they forgot to pay him his fee. In spite of his helpful services he was rather the joke of the community. It is true he was queer, and birds are great gossips, painfully quick to criticize anything unusual. As you have noticed, birds are almost always well dressed, neat and trim in their appearance, and Lawyer Blackbird's awkward figure seemed to them absurd. They made rather cruel fun of him. When he went strolling thoughtfully about in the cool early morning, looking for his breakfast, a mischievous thrush would dart down in front of him and snatch up a worm or insect right from under his beak. They played practical jokes on him, stealing the caterpillars that his clients laid by his front door in payment of his services. They whistled mockingly from the neighbouring trees when he was studying, and screamed with laughter at his clumsy way of flying. Handsomer birds, such as cardinals, blue jays, orioles, sneered at his shabby black suit.

The younger set among the robins were most active in teasing him. Young robins are big lummoxy birds, full of high spirits, alert in their movements, proud of their smart tawny waist-coasts, feeling themselves very important. They were greatly amused at the queer blackbird's innocent pleasure in his log cabin. "Yay, Lincoln!" they used to call mockingly when he came out of his little home for a breath of air. "Yay, Lincoln!" And other birds, birds of no importance, sparrows and young pullets and chattering jays, took up the impudent cry, "Yay, Lincoln!"

Of all birds, baby robins have the hardest time learning to fly. They cause their mothers much anxiety, for they are very fat and also very reckless. Before their wings are strong enough to carry their heavy bodies they often get themselves into positions of great danger. So it happened one day that while Mrs. Robin, who lives in the dogwood tree opposite the dining-room windows, had gone down to the drugstore, young Pudgy Robin, not yet properly able to take care of himself, flopped lumpily to the foot of the tree. It was very thrilling to be out on the open grass, and the first thing anyone knew he was hopping and exploring across the croquet ground. He was interested in the wire hoops, and tried to flutter up to perch on one, but fell off. He was as fat, awkward and helpless as only a young robin can be.

The croquet court is a bad place for a young bird. Anything moving on that stretch of grass is in plain view to many watchful eyes. The cellar doors, slanting up from the ground, overlook it and are the favourite sunning place for cats. And there lay Taffy Topaz, the big yellow Persian. He noticed that hopping bundle of feathers. His eyes got wide and bright and dangerous. His tail switched nervously from side to side. He crouched so that his shoulder blades humped up, and watched intently. Then he began to crawl silently across the lawn. Suddenly it seemed as though the garden was very still. In all that quietness of yellow sunshine there was only Pudgy Robin, blundering bravely into a strange big world, and the creeping enemy behind him.

Then in the treetops the bird policemen began to scream. Little happens on the ground that the bird policemen don't see, though they can't do much about it. "Look out, look out!" they called wildly. But Pudgy was too young, too excited, too ignorant, even to know what they were saying. Not far away was a blue croquet ball that had caught his eye. It would be a fine thing to hop on and look round. He fluttered and tumbled along.

The birds were all screaming in panic, but no one seemed to know what to do. The noise brought out Lawyer Blackbird, who came to the door of his log cabin. One look of his shrewd eyes showed him what was happening. He wasted no time in screaming. Straight as an arrow, on his long wings, he launched himself. He flew, like a flash, right past Taffy's nose. Taffy, whose attention had been all on the helpless robin, was startled and frightened. He glared round in wonder. Blackbird wheeled, flew back again, and hovered in air just above the cat. Taffy sprang for him, forgetting all about the robin. Fluttering in pretended distress, always just beyond the reach of those sharp claws, Blackbird led Taffy away toward the other side of the house. Two big robins, now the danger was past, came squawking and hustled Pudgy to his home tree. When Taffy Topaz saw how he had been tricked he crept back to the croquet ground, but it was empty. Lawyer Blackbird flew to the log cabin and went on with his study.

There is no heroism birds respect so much as the courage that outwits a cat. That day there was no whistling to bother Blackbird at his work. But there was a great deal of conversation in the big oak tree which is the birds' clubhouse. They knew now that Blackbird, though his ways might be queer, was worthy of his log cabin.

They made their plans secretly, so the next day the lawyer was completely surprised. He heard a whirr of wings outside the cabin, and thinking it might be a quarrel of some sort for him to settle, he came outside. There were all the robin policemen, saluting him, and a magnificent air parade. It had all been carefully thought out. First came a squadron of tanagers, all scarlet. Then Mr. Hopkins's white pigeons. Then the blue jays. Red, white, and blue, they flew brilliantly in formation, and wheeled and hovered in front of the tiny log cabin to do it honour. And then Mrs. Robin herself, with tears in her eyes, brought three feathers, one red, one white, one blue, and placed them, like a banner, on the birdhouse of Lincoln logs.

That was in the summer, but the birds do not forget. When the autumn came, the birds in the

Election Day parade carried a big sign which said:—

FOR JUSTICE OF THE PEACE
VOTE FOR ABE BLACKBIRD

PAPER DAFFODILS

THERE was once a man who was not clever at growing flowers. I don't know what it was about him that made it impossible for him to have a really nice garden. When other people's rhododendrons were full of big red blossoms, his own never got beyond sticky green spikes. His rose bushes had plenty of buds, but small unexplained insects ate most of them before the petals opened. He tried for years to grow sweet peas, but they did not seem happy. Instead of climbing up like proper sweet peas they lay flat on the ground and tangled themselves nervously together. Their little soft tendrils clutched miserably at each other like tiny hands.

For a while this man thought well of his irises, but dogs noticed them too. From all round the neighbourhood dogs came and lay on them. Dogs love flowerbeds, especially when the earth has been freshly dug and raked. And a young iris, after having been slept on by a heavy dog, is never quite the same. Or perhaps the word would go round among the truck drivers that it would be interesting to drive their great flat wheels over the edge of one of his flowerbeds or grass-plots.

Sometimes, to have a little colour in his garden, he would go down to Mr. Steiger's greenhouse and bring home a lot of flowers already in blossom. Then he hunted for the trowel and the rake, which took some time. He had some very nice tools in his garage, but they were all wandering tools. They did not like to stay in one place. The trowel, when no one was looking, would slip off and lie under a tree somewhere in the back lot. It was a hide-and-seek trowel, and very clever. When he found the trowel (he never did find the rake, not that special little rake he was so fond of) it was getting dark, but he planted the flowers and watered them. For several days they seemed bright and gay, but gradually they dwindled. They got pale and meagre. He had to content himself mostly with pansies and marigolds, because these will flourish almost anywhere.

This behaviour on the part of his flowers rather troubled him. Sometimes he said to himself that it was because the soil was poor. Sometimes he believed it might be that the flowers were offended because he made mistakes about their names. I think myself it was simply because he was the kind of person to whom awkward things happen. You know, some people understand life so well that everything is always all right. Their clothes, their houses, their gardens, their finger-nails, are always neat and well-attended. Their cars are shiny. Then there are other people to whom embarrassing things happen.

Whatever the reason, it was so. He was not clever at growing flowers. There were other things that grew round him plentifully. He was good at raising books, for instance. It was extraordinary. Every day or so a truck would drive up and leave books for him; he didn't even have to pay for them. It was all part of the magic. Books sprouted all round him. Also people who wanted to sell vacuum cleaners or real estate. And as for the telephone: if telephone calls had been flowers he would have had one of the finest gardens in the world.

But in his ragged garden he had done rather

well with his daffodils. He had planted the bulbs too deep, so they were always later than the neighbours' daffies, and every spring he had to scratch away the earth to help them through; but he enjoyed them all the more when they came. Under his dining-room windows, on the south side of the house, they grew and trembled in the breeze. He was so used to his flowers being less beautiful than other people's that he almost imagined there must be some mistake. He would go out to look at them, and say to himself "If they knew they were mine they wouldn't dare be so lovely."

It's hard to know what to do about daffodils. It is true that they are beautiful in a bowl in the dining room, and very likely people drink their milk and finish their spinach better when there are flowers on the table. Yet they are so graceful and perfect where they grow, especially if there aren't very many of them, it is difficult to decide whether to pick them. It is a hard problem, one of those problems that make life interesting.

That was the problem he was thinking about. There were ten daffodils under the dining-room windows. He had watched them growing and the buds fattening, and now they were all in flower.

Should he pick some for the table, or should he leave them there? While he was wondering about this, the problem was settled for him by someone else—as it so often is. He came home late one afternoon, and going round the house to see what everything looked like he was horrified. All but two of the daffodils had been picked. Not only that, two or three of their bright yellow heads, pulled off short from the stalks, lay fading on the ground. Evidently, in spite of all he had said, the children had been at work. He was greatly upset.

He almost rushed indoors to make an uproar, but he paused to consider what was best to do. In the bathroom upstairs he could hear Helen and Blythe cackling gaily as they took their bath; and he knew that Louise, who was a quick undresser, would be already in bed reading *Sparrow the Tramp* or some other favourite book. It seemed a pity to break in upon the cheerful bedtime with a scolding. Daffodils are important, but children are important too. He lit his pipe and walked round the house to think.

The next day was Saturday, and after breakfast he called the children into his den.

"It's a very queer thing," he said. "Perhaps it's some kind of magic; but I was looking at the daffodils and there don't seem to be as many as there were."

Two of the children opened their mouths, and he knew pretty well what they were going to say. So he hurried to go on talking before anyone could say anything disagreeable about Someone Else Did It In Spite Of My Telling Her Not To.

"It appears to me," he said, "that around this house there is something dangerous that happens to daffodils. I don't know what it can be, but we will have to do our best. Here are pencils and crayons and some sheets of thick paper. I want you to draw some daffodils and colour them. We'll cut them out and put them in the ground just where the real ones were."

Helen and Blythe were too young to see in this anything more than a new game, and they were full of enthusiasm. Christopher and Louise looked at each other a bit queerly, and then started to say something that began with a But. Again he hastened to interrupt them.

"Come on," he said. "Let's see how nicely you can make them. Now we'll have a daffodil bed that we can all really enjoy."

They sat round the dining-room table, with a

real daffodil to copy, and for some time there was silence. Presently there was a tap at the big sliding door of the den, and their father arranged his face in an expression of deep thoughtfulness. They came in with their drawings. The paper daffodils were really very well done. It is true that Blythe's were a bit scrawly, and coloured red and blue, but it was not her fault if the older children had been using all the greens and yellows. Helen's were fat and bushy, Louise's tall and wavy. Christopher's were so lifelike that I think he must have been doing pictures of daffodils at school.

They were all cut out very carefully with scissors, and then the planting was done. The wandering trowel was found, and little holes were dug. The paper daffodils were set in a row at the front of the bed, in the best of the earth so they would flourish. They looked very well. Helen's were not quite so bright a yellow. Perhaps hers had grown in a poorer soil; or perhaps Christopher and Louise had kept the yellowest yellow crayon for themselves.

The moist earth was raked and smoothed around them and they fluttered in the fresh April air. Donny, suspecting a festival of some sort, barked approval. They all stood to admire the display, and then the family went on about its affairs. There was something a little thoughtful about Louise's face as she went looking for a cat to hug.

It was rainy that Sunday: driving April rain and gale. For several days the garden was mostly mud, and there were other things to think about. Then, when dry weather returned, a sodden scrap of paper was found blowing about behind the house. It was part of a daffodil, blown clean off its paper stalk. As Christopher truly said when he revisited the place, now the daffodils were "not so realistic." Those that remained were faded and crumpled and smeared.

And then the paper daffodils were forgotten. Months later, raking under the rhododendrons, their father found a piece of one, and a queer little pain ran round in his mind. Donny, who was rooting and grubbing and snuffing not far away, asked him what was wrong.

"Well, Donny," he said, "it's awfully easy to tear up beautiful things, but very hard to put them back."

Donny only grunted.

"Yes," says Christopher, "but you haven't told quite all the story. As soon as the paper daffodils were planted, Donny went and lay on them just as though they were real."

Certainly it was the greatest compliment Donny could pay them.

JACK BEANSTALK AND THE PEA PRINCESS

IN THE world of toys, just as in real theatres, an actor's life is very uncertain. There are long intervals of unemployment, when the Junior Theatre (made out of an old packing-case) stands idle in the workroom. The little marionettes lie in a box in the corner and grumble because they have nothing to do. Summer time, always difficult for actors, is specially hard for the Junior marionettes. The workroom in the garage gets very hot, and their faces, modelled out of paraffin, sometimes melt out of shape. Once, on a very sultry day, before a matinée, Cinderella had to be put in the icebox to keep her in good condition for the performance. The other puppets, who had no such luck, were very jealous. Cinderella's older sisters kept complaining throughout the show that she smelt disgustingly of cheese. The Prince, who had been left out in the sun after rehearsals, had very bad luck. He was a handsome fellow, with bright blue painted eyes. But his nose drooped, his cheeks sagged, his chin slipped. The blue from one eye trickled down almost to his neck. It changed his whole career. When the theatre reopened in the autumn he could never again play parts as a Leading Juvenile. They tried to lift his face but it had fallen too far. He was given skirts and had to be a Wicked Fairy. This was great bitterness to him, and accounted for his success in this new character. The tragedy of his private life gave a fine savagery to his acting.

The marionettes, whose bodies and limbs are cut out of cardboard and cunningly jointed together with loops of string, get very bored in their periods of idleness. They lie all hunched up, just as they have been tumbled into the box, and have pins-and-needles feelings in their legs. But they do not lose heart, for they never know when a spell of business will come. Theatre managers are always temperamental. Suddenly, perhaps on a rainy day, the theatre will be hoisted up onto the workbench for overhauling. The marionettes hear the thrilling click of the little rings on the wire as the curtains are pulled to and fro. Paints and cardboard are got out, there is the excellent smell of turpentine and linseed oil. New scenery is planned.

Is there anything more fun than painting scenery? I doubt it. A back-drop of a dark pine forest, with sunset colours burning between the tree-trunks, is a great favourite. Or a castle, with pointed turrets, outlined black on a mountain top against blue evening sky. These things don't even have to be very skilfully painted: when the theatre is set up in the dining room, and the little bed-lamp that serves as footlights is well adjusted, even crude scenery looks quite marvellous.

And the Junior Theatre is blessed with a Perfect Audience, an Audience that takes art seriously. The stage is set between the sliding doors of the dining room. A steamer rug hung above it conceals the manager and his assistant. It is a typical matinée because the audience is almost entirely feminine. Louise, Helen, Blythe, Bonnie June, Marie, Jean, and Cissie—seven ladies. Johnny Snyder is the only gentleman. Christopher and Buzzy, of course, are behind the scenes. The audience sits on cushions on the floor. The small phonograph plays a nursery rhyme record as overture. The light clicks on, the curtains open. The play perhaps is *The Three Bears*. There is the favourite back-scene, the gloomy forest brightened with slices of sunset. Goldilocks, descending gracefully at the end of her string, teeters gaily toward the little cottage. Even Bonnie June, who is thirteen and getting so long-legged that she takes up a lot of room on the floor, is not yet too old to be thrilled.

So you can imagine what fun it is to be a marionette actor. To enjoy the attentive silence of the Perfect Audience, to feel the strong supporting threads that hold you up and guide your gestures, to hear the voice above you that says your lines, to know that through all the play everything has been planned for you beforehand and you need not worry. Your hands, your feet, your head, all have that comfortable sense of the string holding them up, telling them what to do. It is a fine feeling. No wonder the marionettes, in their gossip about their art, give greatest credit of all to the String.

The chief topic of conversation among the marionettes, while the theatre lay idle that summer, was the love of Jack Beanstalk and the Pea Princess. That Jack should admire the Princess was natural enough: she was a beautiful creature. You remember her story. An old King and Queen sit in their castle late one stormy night and hear a knocking at the gate. All the servants have gone to bed, so the King goes downstairs himself and opens the big oak door. There, draggled in wind and rain and mud, is a lovely young lady, begging for shelter. The old King brings her in, and they dry her off by the fire and give her hot-milk toast. In the conversation she explains that she is really a Princess of high degree.

Naturally the old King and Queen are doubtful. What would a Princess be doing wandering about like that at night? So when the Queen goes to fix the guest-room bed she slips a dried pea under the mattress. In the morning they ask their visitor how she rested. Oh, wretchedly, wretchedly, she says; I could hardly sleep at all. She explains that there was something hard in the bed that bruised her black and blue. Then they know she was a real Princess: only a royal person could have a skin so tender.

So that was the Pea Princess. But Jack came from quite a different story. He was just a plain country boy, though brave and steady. He was the boy who climbed the bean-stalk and outwitted the giant. He was not handsome. He tried to pretend it was the warm weather that had lengthened his paraffin face into such a soft and melancholy expression. But it was not the warm weather, it was love.

Jack was too shy to tell the Pea Princess how he felt about her. Besides, he knew very well that they belonged in two entirely different stories, and there is nothing so difficult as getting out of your own story and into someone else's. But it would be silly to suppose that Sweet Pea (as he called her) was not aware of his condition. Even if she had not guessed it, some of the other puppets would have told her. As they all lay there, jumbled together in the box, she could feel his admiring eye always fixed upon her. This was not unpleasant, for young women enjoy being admired. But the truth is, she was so very uncomfortable that she was thinking chiefly of her own troubles. A person so sensitive that even a pea under the mattress kept her awake, naturally suffered terribly in such crowded quarters.

Then one fine day some leading spirit among the marionettes suggested a new idea, that they should put on a play of their own. It had never occurred to them before that they might do this, but after all, why not? Quite a buzz of talk rose from the box as they argued about it. Some refused to believe that it could be done without the Manager to handle the strings. But they decided to try. Stiff from lying idle so long they clambered out of the box and stretched themselves.

The great difficulty was to get their strings untangled. Shuffling round in the box, the delicate threads had got all snarled together. This is quite likely to happen to marionettes unless they are put away very carefully. If the tangle is badly complicated they can never unravel it themselves. They have to wait for the Manager. There was a quarrelsome time while they all pulled and tweaked and twisted. They all had different ideas about what to do with their strings when they disentangled them. Some wound them neatly around themselves, under their costumes, so they would not be in the way. Others carried them proudly, coiled at their waists, like cowboys with lassoes. Much excited they walked to and fro on the stage of the theatre, happy to see it again. The scene happened to be set for the first act of *The Sleeping Beauty*, so they agreed to give that play.

In the long time since the theatre had been used, some of the actors had been lost. Sleeping Beauty was nowhere to be found. The only person suitable to play that part was Sweet Pea. But then, as they sorted themselves out and began to get things in order, came a painful problem. The strings of Sweet Pea and Jack Beanstalk had got so knotted together that they could not be separated. Neither one could go anywhere without the other trailing after. It was very embarrassing. Cinderella's older sisters burst into jeering laughter, and several other puppets whispered unkindly among themselves.

The poor Princess was terribly unhappy. Here was her great chance to play a leading rôle, apparently spoiled by this entanglement. She sat miserably on the edge of the stage while some of the older marionettes tried in vain to pick out the knots with their cardboard fists. Jack, very ashamed, stood as far away as the tether of string would allow, and looked grim. In his heart he was very angry at the careless Manager who had allowed this humiliating thing to happen.

Then Sweet Pea, seeing how wretched he was, did a charming thing. She forgot her own disappointment. With tears still on her pretty little paraffin face she said bravely: "Never mind! Let someone else play Sleeping Beauty, Jack and I will watch. If I had to be tangled up with anyone, I'm glad it's him."

This was too much for Jack. There came to his aid the courage he had once shown in climbing the tall swaying bean-stalk. He seized a pair of scissors and with a quick snip he cut off his own strings. This was the most daring thing that any marionette can do. For all he knew, he might have fallen dead on the spot. The others gazed in horrified amazement. But, except for one sharp twinge of pain, he seemed all right.

Sweet Pea jumped up, radiant. She bundled together the trailing ends of string and hid them under her cape where they did not show. Now all was clear, and they went on with the play.

Jack was not in this performance: his costume as the simple bean-climber was not fine enough for the part of the young Prince who comes to wake Beauty from her trance. So he stood off at one side, behind the wings of cardboard scenery, watching. He was quite content not to be on the stage as long as he could watch Sweet Pea. Also he felt different from ever before. The other puppets had all looked at him strangely when he cut off his strings. It was as though they expected some mysterious doom to come upon him. Naturally this made him self-conscious. But inwardly he felt a happy certainty. He was trembling with a new lightness and freedom.

Sweet Pea surpassed herself in this play. How beautiful she was! Some of the marionettes, unaccustomed to acting without any Manager to control them, were awkward and clumsy; they tripped over their strings, forgot their lines, caught their feet in the slits cut for the scenery. But Sweet Pea was perfect. There seemed unexpected grace and meaning in her proud easy ways. In the scene where she goes exploring in the old forbidden attic, and finds the spinning wheel, and pricks her finger, she was thrilling. Her acting was wonderful when she pretended to feel the magic swoon coming upon her. While the Wicked Fairy cackled in triumph Sweet Pea tottered to the window and looked wildly out.

"Will no one save me?" she cried. "In all the sweetness of my youth, must I yield to this cruel spell? Wicked Fairy, you laugh too soon. I *shall* be saved!" And then she sank motionless on the couch.

Jack, watching from offstage, was deeply moved by this scene. He had watched her pale face, and it seemed there was more than just acting in her look. Also, he suddenly thought, if she had to sleep a hundred years it would surely be fatal. She, so gently bred that only one pea under a mattress could bruise her, how could she survive a whole century on that rickety old couch?

The other actors were already crowding into the wings for the end of the scene—the King and Queen, the fairies and maids of honour. But Jack strode through them, shoving aside the gaily-dressed puppet who was to be the rescuing Prince of the last act. He felt a strange sureness he had never known when there were strings to guide him. Almost afraid that she had really gone into a hundred-year trance, he leaned over the Princess and touched her gently. She opened her eyes. To the horror of all the other marionettes, whose sense of artistic propriety was outraged, she sat up and held out her arms. They rang the curtain down at once, but it was too late. Already she was in his embrace.

They got out through the back of the theatre while the indignant puppets were still gaping. "Be careful of your strings," he said. "They're coming down."

"As if I cared!" she whispered to him. "Here, I'll show you." She seized the scissors.

Two little tangles of threads, all knotted together, lying by the stage door, were all they ever found of Jack and the Pea Princess. All sorts of rumours went round among the marionettes, and the old King and Queen, who had found her that wet night outside the castle gate, said they had always suspected she would come to no good. But it's my belief that you'll still find them, somewhere in the vegetable garden, keeping house very happily at the top of the tallest bean-pole.

"I never was much of an actor myself," Jack says, "but you should have seen my wife when she was on the stage. She might have had a great career . . ."

THE UNAMIABLE CHILD

BUDGET, the teddy bear, had been left out in the rain; and you know how wet a large, fat, fleecy, stomachy bear can get. So he was pinned up on the clothes line to dry.

The easiest way to fasten a teddy bear to a clothes line is to pin him by his ears. So there he hung, with the forked pegs tightly pinched on his two tender flaps of ear. He was surprisingly patient. His yellow glass eyes looked a bit wild, and his mouth, sewn in black wool, drooped in a mournful curve, and the palms of his muddy paws hung soggy, but for a long while he was silent. Then he could endure it no more, and the animals in the Grape Arbor Tea Room heard him utter a scream of bad temper.

"You make me sad! You make me terribly sad!" he yelled (it was a phrase he had caught from four-year-old Blythe). "I hope you'll all go to Bide-a-Wee! You sit there telling stories, and I'm pinned up by my ears and can't hear a word!"

The animals gazed in astonishment. They had been so busy enjoying their tea and talk it had never occurred to them that Budget might like to hear what was going on. They had never taken Budget very seriously, or regarded him as a real animal. Now they gathered under the clothes line and looked up in concern.

Budget, after suffering so long in silence, was in a fierce tantrum. He hung there trembling with rage. He had caught a cold from getting so wet, the kind of cold that is always referred to as "nasty," and that also added to his irritation. Now he kept shouting out all the rude words he could remember from listening to croquet games. He shouted very loud, too; louder than he realized, for with his ears pinned up he could not hear himself.

"Dumb-bells!" he screamed. "Big simps! Boobs! Poor fish! Haven't you any manners for other people's feelings? My gracious! You just sit there and have a good time and never think about me. Roughnecks! You better go to Bide-a-Wee, bettn't you!"

They were all scandalized by this outburst. Donny and Fritz tried to jump up to reach his feet, but the line had been put high on purpose. It was the squirrels who saved the day. Two of them ran out on the rope, one from each end. With their clever little paws they unfastened the clothes-pins from his ears. He dropped onto Donny's broad back, and they carried him over to the grape arbor and propped him in a comfortable chair. A cup of hot cambric tea made him feel better, though his ears were still sore. It was agreed that as he had been so ill treated, a story should be told for his special benefit.

"What kind of story would you like?" asked Escargot, the wise snail who always acted as host at these meetings.

"A story in which children get the worst of it," he said peevishly. "I shall never forget their carelessness in leaving me out in the rain. I do think, after all I've done for them, they might be more thoughtful. Four children have used me to go to bed with, one after the other, all these years. Every night of my life, as soon as they're comfortably asleep, I get crowded out of bed. I'm all bruises from falling on the floor. I hope they'll get punished some day. I hope—gosh, I hope they'll all grow up and marry people who kick in their sleep. Yes, tell me a story in which children get the worst of it."

The animals looked at each other in some embarrassment. They could think of a number of stories of that sort, but it is dangerous to repeat them. For they had all been carefully trained to idealize children, to say of them "they are just little animals." But they knew well enough that children are powerful and uncertain, and that no animal is as full of dangerous energy as a child.

The big gray squirrel who had unpinned Budget's left ear volunteered to tell the story. Squirrels are reckless, because they are so agile and live safely in trees. This one took up a comfortable position on top of the grape arbor, shifted the nuts out of his mouth, and looked sharply round to make sure that no outsiders could overhear.

This isn't really a Roslyn Fairy Tale, he said. It happened in the city. Nothing so scandalous could happen out here. My cousin told it to me, he is one of the squirrels in Riverside Park.

There was once a very small boy called Philip who used to go walking in the park with his nurse. And like all proper boys, he always took along a bag of peanuts to feed the squirrels.

I think that in the beginning the trouble was more the nurse's fault than Philip's. Her father had been in the circus business and perhaps for that reason she had a strong passion for peanuts. As they walked along the streets on the way to Riverside Drive she could not resist eating them, and just to be fair she allowed Philip to have some too. The five-cent bag of peanuts, as every squirrel knows, does not hold nearly as many as it used to in the good old days; and sometimes by the time they got to the park there were hardly any nuts left for the squirrels.

That, of course, was regrettable; but it could be forgiven. Any squirrel can understand other people too having a weakness for peanuts. What was really unfair was that Philip learned that the squirrels were easily fooled by empty shells. It was quite easy to hold out the end of a shell in such a way that it looked like an unopened nut. The hopeful animals would come scampering and this mischievous boy would lure them on until they even climbed up his legs and clustered about his hands. Then they would discover it was only a trick. They would look at him reproachfully with their bright eyes, and he would shout with laughter at their disappointment.

If his nurse had been the right sort, she would soon have taught him not to do this sort of thing. She might have reminded Philip, my cousin said, that in Riverside Park there is the famous little memorial of the Amiable Child, which so many visitors to New York have seen. This very small tomb of a peaceful child, right next to the huge tomb of a very warlike man, General Grant, should have suggested to her that the Riverside children ought all to be Amiable. But she was sitting on a bench reading one of those small newspapers that are so popular in the park. My cousin used to wonder what there can be in those papers that is so nourishing? Evidently they have the same attraction for nurse-maids that peanuts have for squirrels. Anyhow, this

THE HOPEFUL ANIMALS WOULD COME SCAMPERING

shabby behaviour of Philip's went on until all the squirrels knew him by sight. Then he could not hoax them any more. When they saw him holding out peanut shells and calling to them, they paid no attention.

All this did not matter much in summer, when peanuts are plentiful. In summer the city squirrels get probably more nuts than are good for them. That little groaning you sometimes hear in the trees along Riverside Drive at night comes from some young squirrels with stomach-ache, due to an excess of rich diet. But winter came, when peanuts mean much to the New York squirrels. For they have been so spoiled by having food scattered about for them, my cousin says, that they have lost their thrifty habit of storing up a supply for the barren season. And then, when Philip and his nurse still continued to eat most of the peanuts before they got to the park, and still amused themselves by offering the empty husks, it was determined to do something.

The boy and his companion did not notice, as they walked home one snowy dusk, that two watchful gray squirrels were following. Up the steep hill from the Drive, hiding now and then behind the piles of snow along the curb, hurrying into doorways to avoid being seen, darting briskly across streets when the traffic was halted, these two trailed Philip and the nurse. In their handsome gray fur they looked like two small busy postmen delivering letters. In that December season the streets are full of all sorts of cheerful doings and even if the two squirrels were noticed they were merely supposed to be hurrying on Christmas errands. Their sharp little faces were full of purpose, and they followed the unsuspecting pair until they reached the big apartment house on West End Avenue where Philip lived. Even then their task was not finished. They ran up to the top of a tree in front of the building. Swaying about in the bare branches and arguing briskly together, they waited along time. They kept careful watch on all the windows of the apartment house. Then they saw Philip's face appear at one of those windows. He saw them too, and was pleased, for he thought that here were two squirrels who had not yet been fooled. He threw down some empty peanut shells that had remained in his overcoat pocket. The squirrels disregarded this unmannerly gesture, and hurried back to the park.

A few days later it was Christmas Eve. It seemed to Philip that an afternoon had never gone so slowly. Along Broadway the shops were bright with toys and pretty things; as he walked with his nurse he wondered impatiently what surprises he was going to get the next day. He had heard the papery rustle of wrappings in his mother's room, the constant buzz of the doorbell as mysterious bundles were delivered at the apartment. He had no brothers and sisters, so he had no one's pleasure to consider but his own. The nurse kept him out late so that he would be sleepy, and then after a light supper he was put to bed. When he was sound asleep his father and mother began setting up the Tree.

Meanwhile, down in Riverside Park, a remarkable thing was happening. From every corner of the grounds squirrels were assembling at the appointed meeting place—the little rocky hill near 84th Street which is where they hold their parliament. It was an extraordinary gathering. The biggest, strongest, most active squirrels had been chosen. There must have been nearly a hundred of them, they covered the outcrop of rock and all chattered together. On any other evening such a crowd would have been noticed, but on Christmas Eve everyone was busy with his own concerns. Windows hung with wreaths shone in the tall cliffs of building along the Drive, the busses were full of people carrying parcels wrapped in red ribbon, the sky was clear and dark and frosty, all the gaiety of that tender evening sparkled in the air.

The two squirrels who knew the way acted as leaders. At their command all conversation ceased; with well-drilled swiftness the furry regiment set off in column of twos. Their plumy tails flirted with nervous excitement as they advanced, in short quick scampers, along the wall that bounds the Drive. The policeman at the crossing was startled when they approached, but he knew that on Christmas Eve you must not be surprised at anything. He saluted them, and held up the busses while they crossed in an orderly rush. They ran swiftly up to West End Avenue. There, in front of the apartment house, they paused in a long line while the leaders pointed out Philip's window. It was open, as healthy bedroom windows ought to be at night. There was a sharp squeak of command, and the army of squirrels charged upon the tall building.

No one but squirrels could have done it! My cousin, who was one of them, says it was a thrilling sight. Some scuttled up the trees and sprang from there onto window sills; others scaled straight up the front of the wall. They darted in quick zigzags up the face of the cliff, their strong toes took advantage of every little ornament and roughness in the stone. The sills were slippery and required careful going, but these were the picked athletes of all the Riverside squirrels, and they were lean and agile with winter hunger. Before you could have guessed what was happening the whole pack had swarmed up to the twelfth floor and entered through Philip's window.

There lay the Unamiable Child, fast asleep; and there in the next room was the beautiful Christmas Tree. Parents and nurse had trimmed it well and gone to bed exhausted. From every fragrant bough hung tinsel ornaments, peppermint canes, cornucopias, coloured bulbs, popcorn strings, shining trinkets. It is sad to have to tell it, but the angry squirrels made short work of that Tree. The Star at the top they did not touch, for squirrels respect the Christmas Star as much as anyone; and the glass and tinsel decorations didn't interest them; but everything else they raided to their hearts' content. They stripped the tree of everything eatable, they hung the popcorn strings out of the window to make a rope by which they could get down again. Imagine their pleasure when they found a large box of peanut brittle underneath the tree. Among so many sharp teeth it did not last long. They did not care much for the sweet part, but they carefully ate out every peanut imbedded in the candy and left the box a mass of sticky crumbs.

They worked quietly and fast. If anyone heard the rustle of their movements he would have thought it only the secret wrapping of packages. They did not bother the presents piled beside the Tree, for they did not want to spoil Philip's Christmas altogether, merely to give him a hint. Then each squirrel hooked a tiny peppermint cane around his neck. They gave a satisfied look at the devastated tree, then they were out of the window and ran nimbly down the long chains of pink and white popcorn.

There was a silence when the squirrel finished this story. The animals looked at each other rather doubtfully. Only the indignant Budget, still remembering his woes, seemed entirely pleased.

"That's fine, that's fine!" he exclaimed. "An excellent story. I think they let him off very easily. He ought to have been hung up by his ears. That story ought to be printed where people could read it."

But Donny was shocked. "Rubbish!" he growled. "It's a terrible story. It could never be published."

The squirrel twitched his tail anxiously as he looked down on his troubled audience. "I don't know whether it's part of the story or not," he said, "but my cousin added that the squirrels ate the peppermint canes for Christmas dinner, and felt very poorly afterward."

It was left to Escargot, the French snail, who was always tactful, to turn their thoughts into a happier mood.

"The French word for peanuts," he said solemnly, "is *cacahuètes*. Very few Americans know that."

They all burst into a laugh. *Cacawate, cacawate!*

they shouted, imitating his delicate pronunciation. And the big gray squirrel is nicknamed Cacahuète to this day.

A STORY ABOUT BAR BEACH

THE kittens always enjoyed stories about fish. They did their geography lessons much better after Fourchette showed them that the map of Long Island looks a good deal like a Japanese goldfish with a long streamy tail. The bays and harbours on the North Shore make it look, Fourchette said, like a fish that has had several bites taken out of its back. This also was an idea that pleased the kittens. Hops made up a rhyme that he was proud of:—

> Various bays indent our coast,
> But Hempstead Harbour we like most.

Then they were surprised when Escargot explained that the word *indent* really means to put a tooth into.

Fourchette believed that young people should study the geography of their own homes, and make maps of them, so the kittens soon learned how to draw a picture of Long Island. It looked something like this:—

The eye of the fish is Jamaica, where you change trains. The wavy line along the fish's middle is the Motor Parkway. Of course the little square under the tooth-marks is the Roslyn Estates.

Now it is quite true that Long Island does not

look very large on a map of the world, though it is almost always marked. But the place you live in, wherever it is, is always big enough to begin your geography with. Escargot was very fond of pencil-and-paper games, and also very anxious to learn about America; so they used to get out the atlas and have great fun moving Long Island round the map. They discovered, for instance, that if you turn the Island around, and put its nose at the lower end of New York City (at the Aquarium, where a fish's nose would feel quite at home) it would stretch up the Hudson River almost to Albany. And then, going on, they would use Long Island as a kind of measuring stick, and travel across the country. Put Long Island's nose at Albany, then it reaches most of the way to Syracuse. And from Syracuse nearly to Buffalo; and from Buffalo to Ashtabula; from Ashtabula to Sandusky, from Sandusky to Fort Wayne. I am pleased to have it reach so exactly to Fort Wayne, because I had a very good roast-beef sandwich in the railroad station there, late one night, when I was tired and hungry.

When they discovered, in this game of pushing Long Island round the map, that it was about as large as the State of Delaware, they were so excited they wanted to write to the Governor of Delaware and tell him about it. And Escargot was much surprised when he learned that Long Island was almost as big as La Manche, his native "department" in France.

Hempstead Harbour, the one the kittens knew best, is the fourth tooth-bite from the left. And if you look very carefully at their map you will see a little spike sticking out in that harbour. That marks Bar Beach.

Bar Beach is a spit of sand and pebbles that juts out into the harbour. In fact it runs almost all the way across, leaving only a narrow channel between itself and Glenwood Landing where the boatyard is. Once upon a time it was quite a lonely beach. Only a few years ago you could drive along there, to the foot of Beacon Hill, and undress in the old Dodge car, and bathe quite privately. Now the gravel works have made a wilderness of the hillsides, and there is a new concrete road, and Bar Beach is built up with bungalows and bathing pavilions, and anyone who undresses in a car will get arrested. But one reason why living on Long Island is interesting is that you can see it changing so quickly, and changes always make people think. Ten years ago the Roslyn Estates were a forgotten little woodland, almost like the forest of Arden that Shakespeare wrote about. Ten years from now—in 1937—they will be a genteel suburb that shaves every morning.

Bar Beach comes into this story, because Bar Beach is famous for one thing; but you will have to be patient a few minutes to see just how.

There was a man who was particularly fond of the dark. He had a big front porch built on the side of a hill, so that it was high up among the trees, and from that porch, at night, he could see a fine speckle of stars. Every evening before he went to bed he used to go out, like the captain on the bridge of a ship, and make sure that the stars were all right. He did not know much about them, did not even know many of them by name, but still he was pleased that they were there. He liked to see how Cassiopeia and the Great Bear play tag with each other, going round and round the Pole Star. In winter he specially admired Orion with his dancing sprawl across the western sky. He had noticed that a line through Orion's Belt leads to the Dog Star, just as though the Dog was following his master on a leash.

One evening this man had been sitting at his desk for several hours. He went out, about midnight, for his usual look at the sky. If you live in the city you don't think much about the weather, but one of the pleasures of the country is keeping an eye on the changes of wind and cloud. To his surprise, when he went on the porch he found that everything had changed while he had been absorbed in his work. A wet autumn fog had come up, very thick. When he looked off the far end of the porch it was so dark he could see nothing. There were no stars at all. There was the rustle and drip of the wet woods, and far down in the harbour the tugs that tow the gravel barges were whistling anxiously to each other. Somewhere out in the Sound a siren was groaning like an unhappy cow. It was a good evening to be safe at home, and he thought comfortably of his couch in the corner of the room. There he could lie, with a warm light above his head, and read a detective story and perhaps eat a piece of cheese while he was reading. That was one of his bad habits.

But he was sorry not to see the stars. Somehow, while he had been at work he had counted on that last look at the clear sprinkled sky. Rather disappointed he felt his way carefully back along the porch. You always had to be careful on that porch, for the chairs had a habit of shifting themselves round in unexpected places. Also you never knew if a kiddie-car or a velocipede might not leap between your feet. You had to look out for Donny, too, who liked to sprawl in the fairway. Whenever you were groping round in the dark in any place where Donny might possibly be, it was wise to say something out loud, such as "Well, old quadruped, are you right under my feet?" If he *was* there, he would reply with a thumping of his flap-flap tail, and you could steer around him.

Feeling his way back along the porch—and it was *very* dark that night—the man bumped onto a chair that had no business there at all. He was annoyed, because he bashed his shin, and he put his hand down to find out what chair it was. On the seat was a very queer object. It was cool, queerly hard-soft, pebbly or prickly to feel, and of an odd shape with points rather like fingers. It surprised him very much. Feeling it, in the dark, he couldn't imagine, at first, what it might be. He took it indoors to look at it in the light.

It was a starfish—one of those queer little five-pointed creatures you find on the shore at low tide, scattered about like asterisks. The children had been down to Bar Beach that afternoon. It was November, and winter was coming, and they wanted to say goodbye to the beaches they would not visit again until next spring. They had brought home a star-fish.

And then it suddenly struck the man that this was queer. He had gone out looking for stars. He couldn't find any, but there, in the foggy darkness, he had put his hand right on a star-fish—the last thing you'd expect to find on your front porch. Sometimes he remembers that, in nights that are very black and thick. Even if you can't find a star, there may be a star-fish that will do just as well.

Bar Beach will never again be a lonely little bathing place. Along that shore the gravel barges and bath houses and hot dogs and ice cream cones will soon outnumber the clams and the crabs. But as long as the water of Hempstead

Harbour stays clean and untainted, there will be star-fish there for children to find, among the wet pebbles when the tide goes down.

FERDINAND AND THE TASTE FOR CHEESE

WHEN Mr. Mistletoe was born the fairies held a meeting in the good old-fashioned way. And, just as happens in the stories, there was a malicious fairy among them, who was annoyed about something or other, and expressed her feelings by a mischievous magic. "My gift," said this bad fairy, "is that every evening, toward midnight, he shall have an irresistible impulse to raid the icebox. And of the things he will find in the icebox he shall be specially fond of cheese."

The ill-natured fairy's idea was that cheese, eaten largely at bed-time, is indigestible. She supposed that this would keep Mr. Mistletoe awake. But one of the other fairies came cleverly to the rescue. "*My* gift," said this far-sighted spirit, "is that he shall have so excellent a digestion that not even the cheese shall disturb him."

Mr. Mistletoe grew up and fulfilled his destiny, which is simply another way of saying that he was, quite unconsciously, obedient to the commands of the mysterious fairies who had power over him. He did eat a great deal of cheese, late at night; and his digestion was so efficient that he was rarely the worse. All this is just a preface to the real story.

The story deals with a mouse in the pot-closet. The pot-closet was in the kitchen, and the latch was broken, so that the closet door stood a little ajar. This enabled the mouse, whose name was Ferdinand, to go out for cautious expeditions in the dark. It had to be done carefully, for there were many dangers. But Ferdinand had heard rumours, from mice who lived in other parts of the house, that under Mr. Mistletoe's couch, in his study, there were often magnificent harvests of cheese crumbs. That couch, you see, was where Mr. Mistletoe lay, late at night, reading detective stories and munching cheese. He was allowed to do as he liked in that room; no one was even supposed to do any housecleaning there without warning him first. That was a privilege such as few men have; but Mr. Mistletoe was exceptional. Mrs. Mistletoe was very patient with him.

Ferdinand, therefore, having heard of this treasure trove, was eager to investigate. It was not easy. In the first place, it was only when the swinging door from the kitchen into the dining room had been hitched open that he could start in that direction. Many a time the closed door prevented him from getting farther. Even then, if he got safe into the dining room, terrors beset him. Footsteps creaked overhead, Donny breathed heavily, or he fancied he heard a cat. Then he would fly wildly back to the safety of the pot-closet. It is all very well for a mouse to say to himself, safe in the shelter of the oatmeal boiler, that this time he is going to be brave and not let anything scare him. A mouse's legs move faster than his mind: when he hears a sound in the dark house he always runs first and thinks about it afterward. If you are a mouse, that is the safest plan.

One night Ferdinand got safely through the dining room, through the living room, and as far as the door of the study. He paused on the sill, and his small jewelled eyes glittered with excitement at the scene before him. All was plainly visible, for Mr. Mistletoe had fallen asleep with the light still burning—as he often did: perhaps that too was the influence of the bad fairy. Those two large objects overhanging the end of the couch were evidently his feet. But it was the gathering underneath the couch that caused Ferdinand's nose to tremble with desire. It was a kind of picnic. Among several pairs of slippers and a book that had tumbled when their host fell asleep, sat several of Ferdinand's friends, enjoying crumbs of crackers and cheese. They waved to him gaily. "Hurry up!" they squeaked. "It's Roquefort!" Their mouths were so full as they spoke that Ferdinand could hardly make out what they said. But his nose had already explained it to him. Roquefort was the kind of cheese that he favoured most of all.

He was about to dash under the couch and join them when he heard heavy pads on the floor behind him. Donny, roused by the squeaking, was coming in. In another instant Ferdinand's retreat would have been cut off.

He did not wait to argue. With one frantic scurry, he looped out of reach of Donny's drowsy paws and was back in the dining room. But return to the kitchen was impossible. There in the doorway was Fourchette, her eyes green as two starboard lights. The desperate mouse gave a wild leap to the nearest place of refuge. It was the keyboard of the piano. The instrument was open, for Junior had been strumming there after supper; and the music rack was pulled out, leaving a small opening. Ferdinand fled into the inside of the piano just as Fourchette sprang for him. There was a heavy crash of bass notes as she landed fiercely on the ivory keys. Donny growled, Mr. Mistletoe woke with a start. Perhaps he thought it was a burglar, for he went first to the sideboard where the silver spoons were kept. Evidently he was puzzled, for next he went and looked carefully at the piano. Perhaps he decided that the noise was a dream, due to the cheese. But he noticed that the piano had been left open, and he closed the lid and the music rack. Ferdinand was trapped.

Unlucky Ferdinand! At first he gave himself up to despair. The inside of a piano is an uncanny place for a mouse to be lost. How he longed for the comfortable pot-closet, for the oatmeal boiler and the baby's saucepan where he was so much at home. As he ran miserably to and fro among the crowded mechanisms of the piano his paws made queer ghostly shivers of sound on the wires. This angered Donny and Fourchette: he could hear them sniffing and miauling outside. After a hurried exploration of the place, which seemed to him as large and tall as a cathedral, he was convinced that no escape was possible. But then a surprising discovery elated him. The front of the piano was full of crumbs.

That needs explaining. Mr. Mistletoe's love of eating between meals, given him by the Bad Fairy, must have been inherited by his boy Junior. For Junior liked to nibble biscuits, cookies, or a slice of cake, while doing his music practice. The family had all wondered at the queer tone of the old piano. They had supposed that the unusual sound of some of the notes was due to the damp weather; a piano tuner would have been summoned long ago except that Mr. Mistletoe went quite wild at the thought of a piano tuner in the house when he was trying to work. But what the piano really needed was not a tuner but someone to clean out the crumbs.

Ferdinand proceeded to do just that. He made himself very comfortable, and was so busy eating that he almost forgot his dangerous situation.

When, the next day, Junior sat down to strum tunes, Ferdinand was badly alarmed for a while. The noise, heard from inside, was rather terrible, and of course Ferdinand did not understand it. When Junior played the *Star Spangled Banner* Ferdinand was much too shaken to stand up and salute. He supposed it was a very severe thunderstorm, and his whiskers went a little gray with fright. But the playing did not last long, and then he discovered a very generous deposit of fudge crumbs up toward the treble end of the keyboard, and that consoled him.

How long Ferdinand stayed inside the piano I do not know. It must have been several days, for he had time to get quite fat on his rich diet. Then came Helen's birthday (she was six). Mr. Mistletoe wanted to compose a folk-dance in honour of the occasion. He knew nothing at all about music, but he enjoyed sitting down sometimes to play random chords and invent tunes of his own that came into his head. He played very forcibly, with much attention to the bass and a strong foot on the loud pedal.

The tune that he composed for the birthday was supposed to give a suggestion of Helen going upstairs to bed. It began with a series of chords climbing slowly, reluctantly, upward. That was Helen going unwillingly up the stairs, her brown eyes looking sorrowfully over the banisters. Then there was a sudden scamper of music trotting down again. That was Helen thinking of a good excuse for one more return to civilization. There followed a little airy skirmish of melody representing her pleasure at being allowed to stay a few moments longer. Then the tune, very solemnly, pursued her upstairs again to the nursery with strong parental chords, hoisted her into bed with a definite thump, and said "No nonsense, now! Not another word!"

Mr. Mistletoe was pleased with this music. He played it with enthusiasm, and the uproar was so vast that poor Ferdinand was frightened almost out of his wits. He ran wildly to and fro inside, thinking the world was coming to an end. And now he had grown so stout that when he trod on the delicately balanced little hammers his weight made them strike the wires, and dainty trills of sound were added to the notes Mr. Mistletoe was playing. It was really a duet: Mr. Mistletoe outside and Ferdinand inside. The little undercurrent of swift shimmering grace-notes, contributed by the frightened hurry of

Ferdinand's racing paws, gave the tune just the sweet pathos of a little girl climbing reluctantly to bed. But Mr. Mistletoe did not guess this. He took all the credit to himself, and merely believed that he was playing better than he had ever done before. Really, he thought, the old piano is in better condition than I supposed. It's getting back its tone. I do believe I should have been a composer. This is really wonderful! He finished the tune with a rolling volley of harmony and sat back waiting for applause.

To his amazement, although his hands were now off the keyboard, a thin little music went on, streaking runs of notes, twinkling up and down. He stared, and then he pulled open the music rack. Out flashed Ferdinand, and was on the floor with one spring. Luckily the kitchen door was open, and in the twinkling of four feet he gained the safety of the pot-closet.

Mr. Mistletoe was looking the other way at that instant, so he did not see Ferdinand dart out and speed across the room. He often wondered why he could never again play the tune *Helen Going To Bed* with such skill and such a richness of wistful melody. Certainly he never guessed that in a way it all went back to the Bad Fairy who makes both mice and men crave cheese late at night.

Ferdinand still lives in the pot-closet. His adventure cured him of his habit of dangerous roaming. It is just as well, for his hearing is no longer as sharp as a mouse's needs to be. The rolling thunders of sound that he lived with inside the piano made him a little deaf.

THE ESCAPE OF THE PENGUINS

(*A Story for Hot Weather*)

WHEN the kittens were asked what they would like to do when they grew up and had to earn their living, there were two ambitions they often mentioned. Hops used to say he would try to get a job at the Fish Hatchery in Cold Spring Harbour. Going to picnics at Lloyds Neck they always passed through Cold Spring, and Hops would look earnestly at those interesting little pools and sluices where the young fish were bred. It was not certain whether any cats were employed in that establishment, but if there was ever a vacancy—perhaps as a night watchman or something of that sort—Hops intended to apply.

Malta's dream was to work at the Aquarium. She had heard that there was a cat there, and she imagined it must be the pleasantest position in the world. Malta had never seen the Aquarium, but it had been described to her, and it sounded marvellous. All those big glass tanks, with fish as bright and pretty as flowers turning and shimmering in the clear water!

It was very hot weather. It was the weather when Donny's long thick hair has to be cut, and you learn, after much patient work with a pair of scissors, that he is not nearly such a big dog as he seems. He looks rather absurd after a good clip, because you don't cut his shaggy head or his curly plumy tail, and with his body so diminished he looks like a small black and white lion. But he is so much more comfortable that no one minds.

It was the weather when two or three times a day the children put on their bathing suits and spray each other with the hose, and big motor trucks stand dripping in front of drugstores delivering ice cream, and you are surprised to see so many coal wagons going about. Nothing sounds so hot, on a July day, as next winter's coal rumbling into the cellar. And on those blazing days you don't need the gong to call you for lunch, because you hear the jug of iced tea chiming like a soft cool bell when it is carried in to the dining room.

The members of the Grape Arbor Tea Room, fortunate in having such a cool retreat in the hot season, thought of doing something for people in the sweltering city. They had the great idea of inviting the Aquarium Cat to come out and spend a country afternoon. And Malta particularly, who had dreamed of being an Aquarium cat herself some day, was thrilled at the thought of actually meeting such a celebrity.

Fourchette wrote a letter, on her best notepaper, which had a very twirly ornamental F stamped on it in green. It was addressed to The Aquarium Cat, The Aquarium, Battery Park, New York City. It had to be rewritten several times, to get it just right, because they all made suggestions as to the best way to address such a famous person. It said:—

DEAR SIR OR MADAM:

The members of the Grape Arbor Tea Room and Country Day School would be so pleased if you would honour us with a visit. Knowing how busy you must be, and your many responsibilities, we leave the choice of a date to you. In the hot weather we serve a cold salmon salad, with Spratt's biscuits, every afternoon at 4:30. Let us know what day you will come and Donny will meet you at Roslyn station. Donny is a dog, but very understanding. Friday is the best day, the Sea Food Market has everything fresh then. Respectful regards from your many admirers, and enclosing L. I. R. R. timetable, which gives approximate time of arrivals at Roslyn,

Yours,
(MRS.) FOURCHÉTTE.

Fortunately they consulted Christopher about the letter before they mailed it. Because Fourchette, not quite understanding about dollar-marks, had written "We serve cold salmon salad every afternoon at $4.30." She thought that a dollar sign should be put in front of all figures.

Christopher explained the mistake, and it was corrected.

Malta at once asked if she could keep the Aquarium Cat's reply, if one came, to start an Autograph Collection.

After that the kittens hung about the post office until they almost wore out the letter-box opening it. They kept bothering Mrs. Breen by asking her if she was quite *sure* there wasn't a letter. She was almost tempted to write them one herself and put it in the box just to keep them quiet. You see, the Aquarium Cat was so surprised by the invitation that it took him some time to answer. At last a letter came, on official Aquarium notepaper which had little pictures of fish printed on it. It was very carefully written and punctuated. Evidently the Aquarium Cat had taken great pains:

The Aquarium
New York, N. Y.
July 15, 1927.

DEAR MADAM:

In reply to yours of the 8th inst., would say, am very pleased by your friendly invitation and accept same with pleasure.

Am very fond of salmon myself, that will be a treat. If I have any luck will try to bring with me one or two small specimens for your pupils, in the interests of science.

Compliments to your Mr. Donny, you may inform him I will take train arriving Roslyn approximately 4.05 P.M. (Daylight Saving) on Friday.

Yours truly,
(Mr.) JELLICOE.

"What are specimens?" asked Hops and Malta. "Does it mean presents?"

There was great excitement the afternoon Jellicoe arrived. Fourchette and the kittens went with Donny to the station. Meeting trains at Roslyn is always an adventure, for they are real steam-trains with nice old-fashioned hissing locomotives. Waiting by the level crossing you can see the train coming far down the track. A spire of white steam shoots up and you hear the whistle. Then the crossing watchman blows *his* whistle and swings down the black and white gates. Then the gong begins to clang, and the engine rumbles past, and the passengers get off. Stout ladies and children have to be helped as it is a long step down to the ground. It will be sad when Roslyn is a smart suburban station like Great Neck or Garden City.

At first they were worried, because they didn't see a cat getting off anywhere. Then, as they might have guessed, they saw him descending from the smoker, at the front of the train. He was a handsome gray, rather thin. He carried a little wicker basket. Hops and Malta tried to be polite, and restrained themselves from asking if he had the specimens all right. While no one was looking, however, they managed to smell the little basket. Immediately they began to purr.

"You mustn't mention it to anyone," said Jellicoe, when they were in the car, "but I managed to get some small trout from one of the tanks, for you and the children. It is against the rules, but sometimes one is able to make an exception." He opened the basket, and there, carefully wrapped in cool cabbage leaves, were three very tiny fish, about an inch long. Jellicoe had fastened them to little sticks so they could be sucked like lollipops.

Fourchette was greatly pleased, and sucked hers slowly and with enjoyment. The kittens gobbled theirs down at once.

The tea was a great success. Escargot and all the others greeted Jellicoe with respectful politeness. Fourchette had been a little embarrassed when she learned he was a gentleman cat: she had feared he might think it was too forward of her to have invited him. But he was so easy in his manners, so plainly a cat of large worldly experience, that they were all delighted. Even Donny was quite friendly.

Jellicoe ate enormously. He seemed very hungry, and they began to suspect that he did not get as much fish at the Aquarium as they had imagined.

"How nice to be out here in the country," he said, when the cold salmon had been finished. "Of course I had heard of the Roslyn Estates, but I had no idea the neighbourhood was so attractive. This is a very refreshing change for me."

"I'm afraid it must seem very informal, after your important work at the Aquarium," said Fourchette. She had very little idea just what kind of work Jellicoe did there, but she felt certain it was important. "What a lovely place that must be to live."

"Oh, I don't know," said Jellicoe. "It gets

very trying, to see all those fish and never be able to get at them. I would never advise anyone to take up the Aquarium as a career. The smell makes one constantly hungry, and the barking of the seals gets on your nerves. You know, they sound exactly like dogs, and they yelp continually. In fact," he added hastily, suddenly realizing that Donny might be offended, "they bark much more than dogs do. I rather enjoy a nice dog-bark, but it doesn't seem natural coming from a seal."

"But how deliciously cool it must be," said Escargot, who did not enjoy the heat and liked thinking about wetness.

"You'd be surprised to see how many people come in, on hot days, because it sounds like a cool place. In fact, a queer thing happened the other day——"

Jellicoe smiled a little to himself. Evidently it was the beginning of a story, and they all settled themselves to listen.

There were two very small (and active) girls who lived in Baltimore. Their family was a convenient one, for there were not only the two smallandactive girls but they had two parents.

They called these parents Daddy and Mother, but as a matter of fact the real names of the parents were Uncle Felix and Aunt Isabel, and I shall refer to them as such.

Baltimore is a lovely city but in hot weather it is very hot indeed. You will sometimes hear people talk about pavements hot enough to fry an egg on, but Baltimore is the only town I know of where it has actually been done. It was on the pavement just outside Uncle Felix's office that the egg was fried, so you can understand how glad he was to get a vacation.

For their vacation Uncle Felix and Aunt Isabel were going to take the smallandactive girls (whose names were Lannie and Sistina) to an island called Martha's Vineyard. They had read in a booklet that this island was Swept by Ocean Breezes, and they bought their tickets at once. To get there they had to take a train to New York, then a steamer to New Bedford, and another steamer from New Bedford to Vineyard Haven. You will find these places on the map of Massachusetts.

It was a roasting July morning when Uncle Felix and Aunt Isabel, after all the labours of packing up and closing the house, got the two smallandactive girls on board a B. & O. train. Like a wise parent, Uncle Felix did not want to spend all the money at the beginning of the vacation; he hoped to have some left to get home with, after the egg-frying season was over. So he thought it would be better to travel in a day-coach, not in a Pullman. But a parent rarely knows what is going to happen. It was so hot, so dusty, and the smallandactive girls were so lively, so sticky, and so well-sprinkled with soot, that by the time the train had reached Philadelphia Uncle Felix had not only moved them all back to a Pullman car, but had even engaged one of those expensive private kennels called a drawing room where he and Aunt Isabel could conceal the energy of the children from the other passengers.

By the time the train had reached Trenton Junction Lannie and Sistina had three times been mopped down with ice-water in paper drinking cups. By the time the train got to Jersey City they were all rather tired and excited. By the time they had crossed the ferry to New York, and had got the baggage on board the New Bedford steamer, all were ready for some innocent amusement. There were two hours to pass before they need return to the steamer, and Uncle Felix thought it might be cool at the Aquarium, which was not far away.

I well remember (said Jellicoe) when they arrived, because of all the many children at the Aquarium that afternoon those two were the most smallandactive. They both had observant blue eyes, and little cotton pinafores, and large straw hats with little holes in the crown for ventilation. I was strolling about near the turtle tank when they rushed up to me and said I was theirs. Sistina, who was only two and a half, seriously thought I was her own cat from Baltimore, and it was difficult for me to persuade her otherwise. Then Uncle Felix, who had the anxious air of a parent who has been through a good deal, and has more ahead of him, spoke to me very politely. I could see at once that he was a man who understood cats.

"Since you have taken such a fancy to the smallandactive girls," he said, "perhaps you would keep an eye on them for a few moments so that Aunt Isabel and I can look at the fish."

It was not a question of my having taken a fancy to them; it was they who had taken a fancy to me. They were both embracing me at once, and the three of us were all tangled up together in such a way that probably Uncle Felix had imagined I was embracing them. The weather was warm for that sort of thing. But it is part of my job at the Aquarium to be polite to the public, so I assented. While Uncle Felix and Aunt Isabel had a nice refreshing stroll along the cool glass tanks, I took care of Lannie and Sistina.

I knew they would be amused by the penguins. There are two penguins who live in a tiled pool. Unless you are familiar with penguins you would not believe how comic they are to watch. There is a wooden platform in the water, up which they waddle, and then, crossing a gangplank, they love to totter round the upper rim of the enclosure. Crowds of people lean over the low railing, only a few inches from them, but the penguins are not at all shy. They toddle about, skipping over the braces of the railing with an absurd little tripping stumble, quite as funny as Charlie Chaplin.

Lannie and Sistina, climbing up by the railing, were enchanted at the sight of these doddering penguins. And indeed their nice white-tiled pool, like a big bathtub, with the green water in it, was very alluring. Just about that time the seals were being fed, and everyone else went to watch; I was left alone with the two children. Of course I was on the floor, as I am not allowed to jump up on the railings. I was trying to warn them not to climb over too far when Sistina remarked "Take a bath with funny duckie" and slipped inside the rail. Lannie followed her, and the two began trotting round and round the inside rim just as the penguins had been doing.

I looked anxiously for Uncle Felix and Aunt Isabel, but they were over at the other side of the building admiring the Groupers fish. And then, to my amazement, I saw the two penguins, each one wearing one of the children's straw hats, calmly climb over the rail and flop down onto the floor. Toddling about, with their little outstretched flippers and the big straw hats, they looked exactly like a smaller Lannie and Sistina.

About this time Uncle Felix began to realize it was getting late. And just then he and Aunt Isabel felt something cool and moist slipped into their fingers. Looking down, in the half darkness of the Aquarium, all they saw were large straw hats and small dark flippers, which they naturally thought were very grimy hands.

"Oh, here you are, children," they said. "Did you thank that nice cat for showing you the sights? Come now, we must hurry." And before I could catch them they were gone, hurrying out across the Park and into a taxi, the two penguins trotting along with them just like two very tiny children.

I was so afraid that in some way *I* would be blamed for all this, that I kept carefully in the background. But I could see from a distance that Lannie and Sistina were having a grand time. They trundled round about the pool until they were tired, then they splashed into it (it is quite shallow) and floundered about in great comfort. Some of the spectators looked at them in surprise, and went round again to read the sign about Not Handling or Feeding the Penguins: but it was such a warm day, anyone who had doubts probably thought it might be an illusion due to the heat. As for Uncle Felix and Aunt Isabel, they had so much to think about, and were so pleased at the quiet way the penguins sat in the taxi, that they did not look at them carefully until the New Bedford boat had left her pier and it was time to wash the children for supper.

When they found that they had two penguins with them instead of two children, the troubled parents were very upset. Uncle Felix, who had been looking forward all day to the quiet evening on the steamer, with a pipe to smoke and a book to read, at first refused to believe it. He thought that if they gave the two small creatures a good scrub, the dark colour (which he insisted was only the stains of travel) would come off and they would prove to be Lannie and Sistina. Finally he was convinced, and rushed to see the Captain. The Captain refused to put the steamer back, and the most Uncle Felix could do was to send a radio to the Director of the Aquarium. I saw the message when it arrived. It said:

> Fear some mistake have two penguins here see if two smallandactive children left in penguin tank consult Aquarium Cat seven thirty is their bedtime arrive tomorrow.
>
> UNCLE FELIX

The radio operator made Uncle Felix pay for "small and active" as three words although it was carefully explained to him that in that family it was always written as one word.

Of course when the radio telegram arrived the Director consulted me at once, and I had to explain the whole affair. He admitted that I was in no way to blame. The chief difficulty now was to persuade Lannie and Sistina to leave the pool, where they were playing house on the wooden platform. It was their bedtime, so they were feeling specially lively. But my likeness to their own cat in Baltimore was very useful: with me they felt entirely at home.

"There's only one thing to do," said the Director, after sending a radio to Uncle Felix that the children were quite safe. "If they won't leave the pool, you'll have to spend the night there with them. If we force them to come out they'll yell, and keep the fish awake all night."

It was the most uncomfortable night I ever spent. The Director himself served supper for all three of us on the platform in the pool. Lannie and Sistina tried to force me to go bathing with them, but at that I drew the line. At last they fell asleep, clutching me very tight. I wish I knew the address of their cat in Baltimore, I should like to send him a postcard of greetings and sympathy.

Meanwhile the penguins went on with Uncle Felix and Aunt Isabel. They sat up to supper on board the steamer and behaved beautifully; when they were tucked into their berths they slept without any trouble. By breakfast time Aunt Isabel refused to part with them. She took them on to Martha's Vineyard with her, while poor Uncle Felix rushed back to New York by train. He arrived in a dreadful state of agitation and humidity.

The Director was equally upset when he found that Uncle Felix had not brought the penguins back with him. He had had to close the Aquarium to the public all that morning. For, as he said, if he exhibited two quite normal children instead of the amusing penguins his patrons expected, there would be complaints. The situation was painful. At first the Director refused to surrender Lannie and Christina until the penguins had been returned. They got Aunt Isabel on the telephone in Martha's Vineyard: she said that the penguins were so happy there she could not hear of their being taken away. The Director replied fiercely that this was not fair. Children, he said, were numerous, but there are only a few penguins in New York.

While the Director was talking to Aunt Isabel on the phone, Uncle Felix simply seized Lannie and Sistina and ran with them to a taxicab. He hurried them onto a train, and they were in Martha's Vineyard that evening. I hear that they are having a perfectly wonderful holiday. The penguins are delightful playmates. They sleep in the same room with the children, and to see the four go in bathing together is one of the sights of the island. Uncle Felix sent me a post-card saying so.

Even the Director, when he went up to the Vineyard to try to cajole the penguins back, admitted it would be a pity to take them away from a place where they were having so much fun. If only, he says, the smallandactive girls don't embrace them to death.

"But what did the Aquarium do without any penguins?" the kittens asked.

"The Director had to get two more sent down at once from the Bronx Zoo," Jellicoe explained. "They have several up there."

Escargot spoke thoughtfully. "I always imagined that penguins must be very interesting birds," he said, "because a famous French writer, Anatole France, once wrote a book all about them. We must read it some day."

THE STORY OF LOUISE'S GARDEN

OF COURSE it was a great day when we got gas in the Roslyn Estates. But Fourchette still liked to remember and talk about old times before the kitchen was rebuilt and enlarged and the beautiful big gas stove put in. She often spoke of those long winter evenings of her youth, when the coal range filled the kitchen with a warm steady glow. She used to lie, drowsed with supper and comfort, in the corner behind the hot water boiler. Outside there was the frosty song of wind in the bare trees, and the glitter of winter stars. The hours went softly by. Sometimes there was the stir of coals in the grate, the tinkle of a falling cinder as the fire settled itself for the night—like a child turning over and dropping her doll out of bed as she falls asleep. The alarm clock went on steadily with its joggling count, *trickery, trickery, trickery.* Floors creaked overhead, the hot water rustled in the tall boiler. Fourchette lay so peaceful in warm trance that the mouse Ferdinand came out of the pot-closet or an athletic roach emerged from the old sink and waved his feelers at her. She paid no attention. It is good for a cat—or for anyone else—to have long dreamy evenings like that in youth.

She lay so until, about midnight, Mr. Mistletoe would come through the kitchen, wearing his long gray dressing gown, to say goodnight to the furnace. When she heard him go down the cellar stairs she got up and stretched, the graceful curving stretch of a handsome young cat. Donny always followed Mr. Mistletoe, pushing the swinging door open with his heavy body. Fourchette envied him being able to do that. She could not go through that door unless someone opened it for her. She had a trick of going through with Donny, slipping under his legs as he pushed the door, which always made him furious.

She and Donny would sniff at each other a little suspiciously, in the dark, until Mr. Mistletoe returned from the cellar. Then, as he moved to and fro getting out some supper for all three, they would both rub against his legs. Fourchette particularly was so clever at getting between his feet that he often tripped in his long dressing gown and had to make absurd skips and capers to keep from falling. Fourchette was a very young cat in those days, and had not really learned that feet are dangerous.

But then came the exciting summer when the Gas actually arrived. Harry Smith and his carpenters and Mr. Penny and his plumbers came to remodel the kitchen. There was crashing and hammering and dust and confusion. The faithful coal range that had cooked so many good meals was taken in pieces and put out by the back steps. It stood there a long time, rusting in summer showers, until someone could be found to take it away. The old boiler that had heated the water for so many grimy children's baths was given to Mrs. Spaniel, the washerwoman, who needed a bigger boiler for washing so many clothes.

What a time it was! It seemed to Fourchette that the strong foundations of life itself were shaken. The stove, the boiler, the good old kitchen sink, were lying about by the back steps. Cockroaches were homeless. Perez, the Filipino cook, had need of all his good humour: he had to do his cooking on an oil stove on the kitchen porch. Because of course the Gas was not ready to go in on the date appointed, and there were several days when the family lived chiefly on cold boiled ham. But at last the pipes were connected, and the new shining gas stove installed. When the burners were lit for the first time all the animals gathered by the back steps and gave a cheer. The workmen from the gas-office in Port Washington were much surprised.

Perhaps the most thrilling part of all this affair was the tearing-down of the old kitchen chimney. Mr. Mistletoe had long been worried about that chimney, which was very tall and slender and supported by iron braces bolted to the roof. It looked dangerous, some of the bricks were loose, and they were glad to have it removed. But what a mess when they began battering it down and bricks and mortar came tumbling into the garden. And, as if there weren't enough happening anyway, Mr. Mistletoe had chosen just that time to have a new sleeping porch built, and the back lawn was piled with lumber and boards of all sizes.

Not long before this upheaval Louise and Helen had suddenly decided to have gardens of their own. They dug up a patch of earth and bought a packet of seeds. They bought zinnias, because the picture on the seed-packet looked so pretty, though not any prettier than the young gardeners themselves bending and raking and arranging a border of stones. But once dug and planted the gardens had been rather neglected, except by Donny who evidently thought them twin beds and slept in them by turns. Blythe, learning to ride a velocipede, used to trundle through them. In fact, few people realized that they were gardens at all; they simply thought them two more patches where the grass hadn't happened to grow. So, when the workmen were looking about for a convenient place to pile the bricks from the kitchen chimney, they dumped them all on top of the two gardens.

I don't think the gardeners worried much about this, for now so many interesting things were happening, and the zinnia seeds, still underground, said nothing. But presently Mr. Mistletoe, who had plans of his own for those bricks, hired Christopher and Buzzy to help him (at the rate of one cent for every twenty-five bricks) and they stacked them up neatly against the side of the garage.

Helen, by this time, had abandoned any

thoughts of raising flowers; but Louise, remembering the picture on the seed-packet, tidied up her patch once more. It looked a bit bruised, but she swept away the brick-dust and poured several cans of water on the earth to encourage the zinnias. Now the garden looked like a small accidental mud-hole, and the workmen, wanting somewhere to pile all their lumber, thought that was the obvious place. Once more Louise's zinnia-bed was covered up, this time with masses of beams and boards, where the workmen sat cheerfully in the sunshine eating their lunch. Donny and Fourchette too lay about on the warm planks, with that enjoyment that all animals have in watching work going on.

So, in the general hullabaloo of tearing down and building up, Louise's garden was quite forgotten. But there was something obstinate about those zinnias. You'd have thought they were poison ivy, the way they hung on. For one day, in a chink among the litter of boards, what should stick up its head but a bright scarlet flower. Everyone was amazed. It didn't last long, though, for in shifting off the planks it got bashed.

Perhaps there was something queer about the

particular spot that Louise had chosen for a garden. Perhaps there was some special luck about it that attracted dogs and cats and velocipedes and workmen. But what happened now was most curious of all. Mr. Mistletoe and Perez had been cutting down trees in the back lot. One of these trees, tall and very straight, had been trimmed and stripped of its bark and sandpapered and varnished. One day, while Louise was away on a picnic, a deep hole was dug and the new shining pole was put up. Of course you can guess what happened. The place where the pole was set was the exact spot where the unsuccessful zinnia garden had been. When Louise came home that afternoon she forgot all about the bad luck she had had. For a surprising flower had shot up, bigger than any zinnia, brighter than any picture on a seed-packet. Tall and straight and clean, the stalk rose thirty feet into the air. At the top was the gayest and prettiest of flowers. Brilliant with colour, it floated gently in the breeze—the American flag.

Probably no one except Louise remembers the courageous little zinnia that once grew where the flagpole now is. But the old kitchen chimney has its memorial too. Mr. Mistletoe took all its bricks and built them into a wall at the back of the croquet ground. He was not very skilful mixing mortar or laying bricks, and all the carpenters and everyone else who came to the house gave him all sorts of advice about doing it. They wanted him to use strings and plumb-lines and spirit-levels and get it nice and even. But his idea, which he was a little afraid to mention to more capable people, was that the wall, when finished, should look like a beautiful old ruin, an antique Long Island relic. Well, it does. It has only been there a year, but it looks a century old.

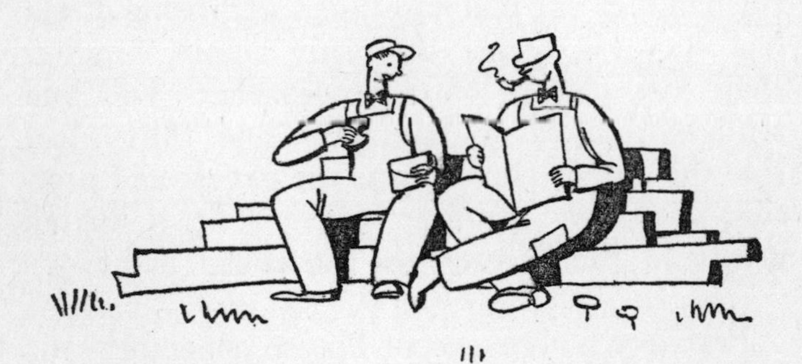

THE PILOT LIGHT

EVEN when you get gas for cooking, that doesn't solve all problems. The gas stove hadn't been put in very long before there was the famous quarrel between the Pilot Light and the Big Burner. They were really rather fond of each other, and secretly each one admired the other's good qualities; but they quarrelled terribly!

You know what a Pilot Light is in a gas stove. It's a very small hidden flame that is kept going all the time for the purpose of lighting a Big Burner when that is needed. You push down a little valve, the Pilot Light shoots out a long streamer of bright flame. It is very interesting to watch. Turn on the gas in the Big Burner, then press the valve. The dainty streak of yellow fire darts from the Pilot like a magic wand: the Big

Burner seizes it and blossoms into a roaring blue flower.

You would have thought the Pilot Light would be rather proud of itself, pleased to have such fairylike work to do. Perhaps the trouble was that the other burners had teased it a little too much; perhaps, like many people with magic powers, it was temperamental. It had a fiery nature, which after all was not surprising. You know how in the old stories there is often a fairy who has a habit of imagining that she has been slighted or disregarded or offended in some way or other. It was like that with this clever but rather foolish Pilot Light. It was terribly jealous of the Big Burner. It complained bitterly of having to work all the time while the other burners were resting. It was even ashamed because its own flame was tiny and yellow while the Big Burner was so large and blue and powerful; it was annoyed that the Big Burner got all the fun and glory of cooking the food.

So the Pilot Light sulked in its little hole at the back of the stove. While the Big Burner, too busy to think about such differences, was blazing away, cooking soup or frying eggs or heating cocoa, the Pilot Light grumbled and whined and was sorry for itself. It never stopped to think that though the Big Burner did a lot of loafing, also when it *did* work it worked furiously. The Pilot Light was so sensitive it imagined that everyone was making fun of it. When it heard all the pleasant sounds of cooking, it thought the others were mocking it. There was the bubble and hiss of water steaming in the big white kettle, the bump-bump of potatoes joggling in the boiler, the sharp snapping of frying bacon, the gentle simmer of vegetables stewing in pots, the deep rumbling crackle of the oven below them all. And these voices seemed to the angry Pilot Light to be saying: "You silly little drudge! Working all the time! Only useful to light up the Big Fellows and let them get all the fun and glory! Just a kind of office-boy! *You're* not much!"

One day the Pilot Light was so indignant that he simply went out, quit. The family had got so accustomed to depending on him that there were no matches at all in the kitchen. Mr. Mistletoe, who always had matches in his pocket, was away that day. No cooking could be done until they had gone next door and borrowed some matches from Mrs. Hopkins.

The Pilot Light was so peevish that he stayed

out for several days. He made trouble, too, because when he was not burning there was a nasty little smell of gas in the kitchen at night, which gave Fourchette a headache. The gas-man came and fixed him so that he had to burn whether he wanted to or not. This made him grumble more than ever.

Then something happened that taught the Pilot Light a lesson.

One winter night there was great anxiety in the pot-closet. Ferdinand, the mouse, was grown up now, and he and his wife Isabella had a family of baby mice. If you have ever seen very young baby mice you know how pretty and quick they are, and can understand that their parents think highly of them. And one of these young mice had got bronchitis. It had gone down into the cellar, which was forbidden, and had got its feet wet in one of those puddles that appear after a heavy rain, and now it was very ill. It was very ill indeed: it had a high fever, its soft fur was all rumpled, its poor little pointed nose was burning hot, its pink patty-paws were shivering cold, it had a pain in its chest and could hardly breathe. It was very patient and lay without complaining in the custard cup that Ferdinand

and Isabella used as a nursery, but its eyes were bright with fever and Ferdinand was very anxious. Suppose bronchitis should turn into pneumonia? It was chilly and draughty down in that corner of the pot-closet. There was only one thing to do: the sick mouse must have a hot compress on its chest immediately.

But how was anything to be heated, in the middle of the night? In this dreadful difficulty Ferdinand did what he would never have done except in case of necessity. He took a small drink of brandy from his flask, to encourage himself, then he put up a flag of truce and went boldly out into the kitchen to ask Fourchette's advice. He knew that Fourchette was a parent herself and would put aside old quarrels for the sake of a sick child.

Fourchette was certainly surprised to see Ferdinand (his whiskers trembling a little with nervousness) advance with a flag of truce. But she was always well-bred, and said politely but with a small touch of mischief, "It is a long time since I've seen you."

Ferdinand explained his anxiety, and at once Fourchette suggested the Pilot Light. Burning there quietly at the back of the stove while all the house was asleep, it was just what they needed.

They had to call Donny, and Fourchette gave him the Flag of Truce call which means This is an Emergency, All the Usual Rules Are Suspended, This call is four quick burrps: a burrp, as you know, is a sound in between a purr and a miow. Donny came hurrying and opened the swinging door so that Fourchette could go through. She rushed upstairs and got camphorated oil from the medicine cupboard and a doll's saucepan from Helen's doll-house. She brought these to the kitchen. Donny allowed Ferdinand to jump on his tall back and from there onto the gas stove, which was all cool and comfortable except just in the little circle over the Pilot Light. There they heated the camphorated oil and carried it to the pot-closet. Ferdinand rubbed the baby mouse's chest with it, and Isabella fixed a little bandage.

All that night Ferdinand was busy, running between the pot-closet and the Pilot Light, heating camphorated oil. Fourchette bit off pieces of dish-cloths to be used as compresses. They mixed a little mustard with the oil, to make a kind of plaster. Ferdinand knew, from long experience, where all the groceries were kept. The Pilot Light burned steadily and all went well. Towards morning the sick mouse showed a healthy perspiration and fell comfortably asleep. The fever was broken. They covered him over with a warm blanket of Corn Flakes and left him to rest.

The Pilot Light bragged about it next day. If it hadn't been for me, he said, that mouse would have died. This was quite true, and it gave the Pilot Light quite a new idea about his importance. He was no longer unhappy because he had to be ready for action at any time, day or night. He saw how silly it was to be jealous of the Big Burner because the latter is stronger and hotter and has a more showy job. And nowadays, when the Pilot shoots out his thin yellow glim, and the Big Burner catches it and leaps into a roaring circle of blue fire, each of them respects the other for his powers. "Thanks! Good kid!" says the Big Burner in his hoarse blustery voice. "Now watch me boil these potatoes. I'll make 'em bobble!" And the Pilot Light, as he flits back into his little socket, calls in a merry squeak "Go to it, Big Boy! I'll be here when you need me."

Mr. Mistletoe heard about all this later, and cheered the Pilot Light a great deal by something he said one evening while he and Pilot were getting ready to start the Big Burner on some midnight cocoa. "You see," he explained, "you're really just like an Editor running a magazine. He won't ever get as much praise as the people who write stories for his paper. He's all the time lighting up burners that are bigger than himself. But they know, and they don't forget, that they got the spark from him."

GISSING POND

SOME of the best evenings the Grape Arbor ever had were when the Gissing Pond Quartette came up to sing. The frogs of Gissing Pond are famous singers: every year for I don't know how long they have won the championship —not only over the frogs from the other ponds in the Roslyn Estates, but in the big competition between the Village and the Heights. You know what rivalry there is between our two fire departments, the one in Roslyn and the one in the Heights, to see which can get to the fire sooner; and between our two post offices, to see which can sell more stamps. Well, it is just like that among the frogs. Every spring is the big Choir

Festival. From every pool in all our woodlands, from the smallest green swamp in the Estates as proudly as from the famous Mill Pond, frogs come hopping down to Cedarmere, the beautiful old place by the water where William Cullen Bryant lived. There, by kind permission of Mr. Godwin, they sit on the stone bridge across that picturesque lake and sing their competitions. Big snapping turtles crawl up on the bank to listen, herons and muskrats and wild ducks applaud from the reedy shore of the harbour.

The Gissing Pond Quartette always wins. (Mr. Godwin's white ducks are the judges.) When the Quartette whistles a light airy wheedling tune like *Over the Hills and Far Away* it is enchanting. When they troll the old Scotch ditty *Roslyn Castle* (from which Roslyn takes its name) the echoes repeat it all down the harbour as far as Bar Beach. Then they pitch their voices very low and sweet and break into *Drink to Me Only with Thine Eyes*. Basso, the big bullfrog who sings the bottom notes, has a thrilling throaty rumble. To hear his deep bass sliding under the others, supporting and completing the harmony, brings tears to your eyes. When they finish that song there is the finest applause of all—perfect silence.

The Gissing Pond Quartette will always win as long as they have Basso. He might have been a very famous singer, for he was often urged to go into Grand Opera; but he preferred the quiet life of the Roslyn Estates. He is a plumber by trade, very clever at mending drains and fixing leaks or anything wet. He sings only to give his neighbours pleasure.

One evening when all the animals and children were in the arbor, and the Quartette had sung for them, Escargot asked Basso very politely if he wouldn't give them a few reminiscences. Basso is an old-timer, very large and stout. He is always pleased to be asked about Roslyn history.

"I don't suppose any of you," he said, "not even Bonny June who is the dean of the children in our neck of the woods, really remember Gissing Pond as it used to be in the old days. It didn't even have a name then, it was just a pond in the wilderness. Concealed in the hollow below the old ruin, behind big trees and the tangle of blackberry briars, few people knew it was there. I remember Mr. Mistletoe's excitement when he first discovered it. He had been brought up to believe that children should always have a tadpole pond handy: what luck to find one almost at your front door! He used to come and sit on an old stump and smoke his pipe and wish the children would hurry up and grow big enough to hunt tadpoles. I was a tadpole myself at that time, and it rather worried me.

"When I consider that my family have lived here for so many generations—even before the Union Mortgage Company—it amuses me to think of Mr. Mistletoe feeling so proprietory about our pond. He always had a comic belief that he was a pioneer in these parts. He used to say, 1620 the Pilgrims settled in New England, 1920 the Mistletoes settled in the Roslyn Estates. But I have a kindly feeling toward him, because, though it is not generally known, I actually lived in his house for a while. He couldn't wait for the children to grow up to the age of tadpole-hunting so he went in wading and caught some himself. I was one of them. He put us in a milk bottle and took us home with him. He said it made him feel young again to have tadpoles in the dining room. I was afraid he meant he was going to eat us. But apparently he regarded us merely as a decoration: we were kept in a bowl in the dining-room window for some time. Then, when our legs began to grow, he took us back to the pond. That was kind of him, and I have always been grateful. Therefore I am pleased to come up here with my friends and sing for you."

Basso cleared his throat and sat thinking in silent dignity. He is rather a pompous old fellow, and they have all learned that he likes to be treated with deference. They sat waiting respectfully for him to proceed.

"Yes," he continued, "you are all too young to remember those days properly. But it is a very good thing for children to have some one place rooted in their early memory: a place they know by heart and whose traditions will always be dear to them. Even for kittens it is a good thing to be respectful to their elders," he added sternly, noticing that Hops and Malta were a bit frolicsome.

Fourchette cuffed the kittens into order, and Basso went on.

"I recall my father telling me about the first night the Mistletoes ever spent in this house. One of the vans bringing the furniture broke down on the way, and the family had no beds to sleep on. Louise, who was only seventeen months old, slept in her baby carriage in the room which is now Mr. Mistletoe's den. Louise was a very wriggly infant, and she had to be strapped in."

All the animals looked at Louise when her name was mentioned. Pleased and yet embarrassed to be singled out in this way she squirmed violently and looked wildly at the sky in a sudden fit of bashfulness.

"Where did *I* sleep?" cried both Helen and Blythe.

"You? Why neither of you were born or thought of," said Basso severely. "Helen might have been thought of, but certainly she hadn't been born."

"How about me?" asked Donny, who is now the senior dog of the Roslyn Estates and thinks himself rather important.

"You didn't exist either," said Basso. "Why even Gissing, the dog our pond was named for, wasn't born till that autumn."

"I don't believe the old frog was born himself," Donny grumbled irritably to Fritz in a hoarse whisper. "He's an old windbag."

"Mr. Mistletoe slept on the dining-room floor that night," Basso told them. "He left the light burning all night so that if the van arrived in the dark it could find the house. The frogs could see the light through the trees, and sang extra well, that warm spring evening, to make a good impression on the newcomers. Mr. Mistletoe was astounded at the beauty of their voices. That's how he first knew there must be a pond near by. As soon as they got the furniture into the house, next day, he went out to explore. He discovered the pond, and what times they had. The first violets always grew there, and Christopher had to teach Louise to pick them with their stalks, not just to pull off their heads. There were picnics in the long grass, and turtles in the mud, and a huge old fallen willow tree where you could play house. I'll admit that for a while we didn't care much about this new invasion. My father put up a sign NO TRESPASSING, but that family never paid any attention to Private Property signs.

"It was a few months later that the dog Gissing appeared. The furnace man brought him up from the village in his pocket when he was just a tiny puppy. I never had any use for that dog myself. He was terribly excitable, and he was mad about the pond. Every day, on the slightest possible excuse, he was down by the water barking, snouting and snuffling about in the mud and bushes, plunging in to chase sticks that were thrown, churning to and fro in the water and making a hideous clamour. Some of our oldest frog families couldn't stand it at all. There began to be nervous breakdowns among the tadpoles, and they moved away to new homes. I never approved of the pond being named for Gissing. He was a wild noisy fellow, and I can't understand how he became so famous. We were well rid of him."

"What became of him?" asked one of the younger animals.

"He snapped at some of the neighbours' children and he was taken to Bide-a-Wee," said Basso, and there was a thoughtful silence.

"It may not have been altogether his fault," the old frog added. "Mr. Mistletoe put him into a book, and it went to his head."

"Don't let's any of *us* get put into a book unless we write it ourselves," said Donny anxiously. "Then we can really tell the truth about things."

"Well, Gissing Pond went on in its quiet way," said Basso. "In winter they used it for skating, it was as good as having a private rink. There were snow-shovelling parties, and bonfires on the shore of the pond, and little star-patterns on the clear ice where the children had sat down hard. Mr. Mistletoe used to bring an axe and chop up limbs of dead trees to take home for his fireplace. Dame Quickly, the old Dodge car, often drove right down to the edge of the pond so that he could load her with firewood. New houses were built not far away, but all the frogs got together and made such queer noises at night that people were afraid to come and live in them. We sang the Mortgage Song, which always alarms people when they hear it sung at midnight in a minor key. The magic of the place was strong, and it kept its perfect loneliness. But then one day an amazing thing happened. Perhaps we had sung the Mortgage Song too loud, and aroused some realtor's resentment. The pond disappeared."

"Disappeared?" exclaimed some of the animals, greatly shocked, while others, who knew about it, nodded their heads.

"Absolutely disappeared," repeated Basso solemnly. "We haven't quite got over the shock of it yet. Some workmen came one day, and dug a trench, and in a few hours the water all ran out. It drained down into that other pond, across the Mineola Road, and left only a big mudhole. When Mr. Mistletoe came down he was dreadfully upset, he walked about like a man in a daze.

He thought the pond was gone for good, and I saw him pick up a pebble from the mud to keep as a souvenir. He told me he was going to keep it with the pebble Captain Bone gave him that came from the middle of the Atlantic. He thinks there's something amusing in having those two pebbles side by side: one from the bottom of the Atlantic Ocean and one from the bottom of Gissing Pond.

"The frogs were badly startled too, I can tell you. Some hopped over to other ponds, but the rest of us stayed around to see what would happen. And I want to pay my respects to Bonny June and Buzzy, who came to the rescue in that distressing time."

Now it was Bonny June and Buzzy's turn to look embarrassed, and they did.

"Bonny June and Buzzy, like all the other children, had heard the sad news and went down to see. In the very middle of the mudhole they found a little puddle of water left, and in that puddle was a fish. All the other fish had escaped down the trench when the water drained off, but this one, a small perch I believe, had got caught. There he was, very puzzled and frightened, going miserably round his small tepid puddle. Bonny June left Buzzy to speak kindly to the perch while she ran home and got a bucket. They filled it with clean water and put the perch in it and carried him carefully over to the Allens' pond. That was well done, and the Gissing Pond Alumni Association honoured them with a vote of thanks.

"But as you know, things weren't as bad as we feared. It seems that they were only draining the pond in order to clean it, and the real estate men hoped to get rid of that Mortgage Song that was alarming people. A lot of trees were cut down and the shores of the pond were trimmed, and a little grassy walk was planted all around it. I'm afraid they're going to make it civilized, very different from the old romantic spot. But anyhow the water all came back, and we hope for the best. And by the way, one of Mr. Hopkins's pigeons brought me a letter from the perch in Allen's pond. He says he is very homesick, and if Bonny June and Buzzy will come with the bucket he'd be glad to be taken back to his old home. He says he'll wait right by the stone steps at the edge of Allen's pond so they'll have no difficulty in finding him."

It was getting dark in the back lot, time for children to be in bed and frogs in pond. Basso and the other members of the Quartette went hopping down the drive past the traffic lights of the fireflies. When they had crossed the meadow and got into the moist ground near home they paused for a final serenade. Their voices, Basso's deep boom strongest of all, were joined in close harmony. "Good Night, Ladies," they sang in rich tones, with all sorts of humorous trills and variations. The words, in a throaty frog accent, came floating up through the sparkling summer dusk. "We're going to leave you now. . . ." Then, if you had been listening very carefully, you could have heard four cool splashes as the singers dived gaily into the water of Gissing Pond.

RABBITS WITH WET EYES

ONE evening while Mr. Mistletoe was pulling up plantain-weeds. . . .

But before we go on I had better tell you a few details about Mr. Mistletoe's adventures as a grass-grower.

He was always happy when he was mowing the lawn—though *lawn* is certainly too smooth a word for such a bumpy arrangement of ground. There is something very soothing in the whirr of the twirling blades, if it is not broken too often by the hard shock of a stick or a pebble or one of Donny's old bones. Keeping the lawnmower straight, and enjoying the smell of cut grass, and feeling your own strong earth solid under your feet, is a healthy pleasure.

But though Mr. Mistletoe was very happy mowing the grass, he looked serious. Perhaps he was thinking? Certainly there was plenty to think about. I wonder what there was about his ground that made it so attractive to moles. Every time he thought he had got the front grass-plot in pretty good order, there appeared a new lot of their wrinkly little subways. Then these soft tunnels had to be all carefully trodden down or else flattened out with the heavy roller. Worst of all was when Donny and Fritz would decide to give some help in the mole problem. Then, when Mr. Mistletoe came back in the evening, he would find a ragged zigzag furrow, ten or fifteen feet long, dug up one of the terraces; or a hole big enough to bury a neighbour's child in. These excavations were worse to repair than all the tunnels a whole family of moles could make in a month.

Another thing Mr. Mistletoe used to think about, as he went solemnly to and fro with the lawnmower (stopping now and then to light his pipe and wipe his forehead) was the idea of starting a Nassau County Weed Show. In a Flower Show he would have no chance at all; but in a well-conducted Weed Show he ought to get a prize. His plantain-weeds were remarkable, both in number and size. And in a good Weed Show there should also be prizes for the greatest number of croquet hoops lost in one season, or balls disappeared among rhododendron bushes, or velocipedes left out over night. In such competitions, he believed, the family would rank high.

But the plantain-weeds were his special concern. On warm evenings he often spent an hour or so grubbing them up. Sometimes it seemed as though the lawn was really more plantain than grass. But it is quite good fun pulling them up, because you are never sure whether the roots will come or not. If you are careful to get hold of all the leaves, and give a little twist, the chances are that the roots will come too. The game is to keep score, and count how many roots come and how many don't.

What bothered Mr. Mistletoe, in these adventures, was that anything so plentiful as those weeds should be so useless. For he liked to imagine that almost everything is useful in one way or another if you understand about it. It always gave him great pain to throw anything away: he carefully preserved bits of string, heads of broken dolls, small pencils, buttons, corks, rusty nails. He rarely put these odds and ends to any purpose, but it made him happy to have saved them.

One evening, then, as I started to say at the beginning, Mr. Mistletoe was cheerfully pulling up plantain-weeds and putting them into a basket. When the basket was full he carried it into the woods and dumped it, and doing so he had to pass by the rabbit run. As he did so, he always said "Well, bunny bunny bunny," which was not an important thing to say but showed a friendly spirit. He and the rabbits led very different lives, and perhaps they did not really have very much in common, but at any rate they were on good terms. So he was shocked, passing their wire netting, to see that their eyes were full of tears.

They were white rabbits, with beautiful red eyes. Even in their cheerfullest moods there seems something a little wistful about eyes of that colour: they look as though they had been reddened by long and inconsolable weeping. So when you take eyes that are naturally red, and fill them with real tears, the effect is very sad. Mr. Mistletoe was painfully startled and stopped by the netting to wonder.

If he had not been rather a stupid man he would have guessed long before. The rabbits had been trying all summer to tell him, but he could not understand their language. It was gradually breaking their hearts to see him, day after day, pulling up and throwing away the beautiful delicious plantain-weeds they love so much. Among the many things that Mr. Mistletoe did not know was the interesting fact that juicy green plantain is one of a rabbit's most favourite foods. And to remain helpless in their enclosure and watch all that plantain being wasted was more than they could bear.

When he stood there, holding the basket of weeds and wondering, the rabbits became greatly excited. Their ruby eyes glistened with trouble, their tall pink ears quivered, they stood up poking through the wire with noses that twitched.

"Good gracious," said Mr. Mistletoe. "They seem terribly upset about something. Can it be that they want some of the plantain? It might be very bad for them."

It seems queer that a man could be so ignorant. Do dogs like bones? Do horses like apples? Do Chinamen like rice? Do girls like fudge? That is how rabbits feel about plantain.

The behaviour of the rabbits was so emphatic, their eyes were so eloquently wet, that Mr. Mistletoe thought he might give them just one plantain and see what happened. When he began pushing it through the hole in the netting they almost tore it from his hands. They fell upon it like sailors on a glass of grog after a long, long voyage. There was a violent nibbling and crunching and in half a minute that green weed had entirely disappeared, even the little cluster of roots.

Mr. Mistletoe watched anxiously. He had a sort of idea that perhaps Binny and Bunny would suddenly fall dead. But they looked stronger and bigger than ever, their noses trembled with healthy vibrations, the tears had vanished from their eyes. They looked at him in a way he could not possibly misunderstand.

Good heavens, he said to himself, and gave them the whole basket.

Late that night Mr. Mistletoe was waked by

a queer soft cheerful sound coming from the back yard. The rabbits were singing.

Slowly and quietly Mr. Mistletoe thought about this matter. He noticed, after that, that every time he began to pull up plantain-weeds the rabbits were watching him closely. Then a great idea came to him. He hunted about in the attic until he found the old baby-pen that had been used by the children long ago. He carried it outdoors and put it over the richest and thickest patch of plantain on the lawn. Then he put Binny and Bunny in the pen. There was a merry sound of crisp eating, and that was the end of that patch. As they ate, the rabbits' active paws patted down the earth smoothly and neatly so that all was left tidy. After an hour's time he shifted the pen to another place and they began afresh.

So that is how the great institution of Plantain Hour was started. Every summer evening the rabbits have their outing in the pen, and move round from one part of the garden to another. That is why Mr. Mistletoe's lawn is now so beautiful, and why the rabbits are the most buxom in the Roslyn Estates. Just look at them!

And how about the mole-subways that Donny and Fritz dug open? Well, Mr. Mistletoe had learned a great secret. It is this, that grass will always grow excellently in places where it isn't wanted or expected. The stone gutters along his driveway, and the blue gravel of the drive itself, were thick with fine healthy clumps of grass. So he invented the trick of pulling up these little clumps and transplanting them into the ragged holes where the dogs had been at work.

A grass-plot could get the better of Mr. Mistletoe for a while, but it couldn't fool him permanently. In some ways he was quite an ingenious man.

CHICKENS IN THE FIELD

BLYTHE came across the lawn, her hands hidden behind her. Eyes roguish, her small positive person swinging gaily, definitely, in time to the tune she was singing. "I know a secret—I won't tell; I know a secret—I won't tell," she chanted.

Yes, she knows a secret. What is it, I wonder? If *we* knew, you and I, it wouldn't be a secret.

Sometimes I think I have guessed a hint of it—that the age between four and five is the most beautiful of all. I meet her upstairs unexpectedly in the middle of a hot summer night, trotting in her pyjamas. Perhaps she felt a sudden solitude, and planned an emigration into Mother's bed. (Do you know that sound of small bare feet on large bare floors, heard from below?) Or after breakfast when she climbs on a chair by the victrola, puts on a record, and dances to it with solemn grace. Quick, flitting in every movement, a dancing shape, an image gay. "She's always running," said observant Christopher. "She's an awfully quaint little thing."

She knows a secret. There are suggestions of it sometimes in the stories she tells. Riding in the car she feels an urge to narrate. She invents a myth or a long chantey of her own and recites it endlessly—if she can compel the others to silence; not always easy, for they too have epics they hanker to impart. She makes unexpected flashes of utterance, as when Dean Swift, loudly blowing her horn, went carefully round a dangerous corner. "I hear the Dean saying Excuse Me," said Blythe. That clear spring day at Lloyds Neck, when a cold April wind was crisping frills of white broken water along the beach. The whole shore was edged with a pure white band of foam. It was one of those crystal days of earliest spring, too fair for steady thought. She looked at the shining fringe of breakers and heard their clean hiss on the pebbles. (She was only three.) "Snow," she said, "Snow saying, Sorrow to come in."

She knows a secret. Perhaps once we knew it too.

Darker occasions—when there are beans or spinach to be finished. The old family cry: Finach your spinach! Steadfast unshakeable passive resistance. "You make me sad! Do you want me to burst right open?" Very well, Blythe, no chocolate cake if you don't finish your vegetables. A slow steaming of tears in those dark eyes. (And gosh, what eyelashes!) Blythe, go and look at the doorknob, see if there isn't a smile there. There's a glass door-handle, just her height, on a door that has a mirror in it. According to legend a Special Smile lives on that doorknob. The trick is that when Blythe goes there to look for the smile on the knob, she sees herself in the tall mirror behind it. And in her grim unspinachable mood she looks so comic that she herself bursts into a grin. Well then, did you find it? She climbs again, smiling but businesslike, into the high chair. But the spinach is never finach. Ask the dining-room rug.

An idea for you: when you grow up and have children of your own, get a dining-room rug that is spinach-coloured.

The best stories are those Mother tells for Blythe's benefit, coming home in the car. After a long drive, perhaps out Farmingdale way to buy fresh vegetables from the stalls along the road, small passengers get restless and bickerish. I don't know why it is: Mr. Mistletoe has to brood and think a long while before he can tell a story, but Mother can spin a yarn right off the reel. The older children relish those stories too, with all the professional zest of literary critics, for they can appreciate how subtly the fable is adapted to Blythe's requirements, her mood and station in life. One of them is the story of Chickens in the Field. I have never heard it told, only heard it spoken of. As I say, it is Mother's story, and she is the one who can tell it properly.

One of the musics that Blythe makes up for herself, as the car hums along the road, is Chickens in the Field. "Chickens, chickens, in the field," she sings, many many times, to a tune of her own. That is all there is to it, but it goes on for a long while and is a great comfort. The story tells why the chickens were in the field, and what they were doing there.

Once upon a time there was a hen who had a large family of young chickens. They were a great care to her. They had to be watched and looked after all the t me. The hen had to see that their feathers were kept clean, that they drank fresh water, that they didn't get their feet wet, and didn't eat indigestible beetles with stings. This busy hen was on the go all day, clucking to them not to cross the road in front of cars, not to wander into the next-door garden, not to go rambling in the open field which was full of dangers. Like all mothers, her legs got very tired toward evening. But if she lay down a minute to rest them in the nice warm dust, the chickens were in some trouble or other. Shrill peeps of dismay summoned her, and she would run to the rescue, all her feathers trembling with anxiety. Weary as she was, she couldn't get a good sleep at night, with all those soft jostling chickens crowding under her wings and even squatting on her back. I used to see her out walking in the morning with her family, and there was sometimes quite a wild sparkle in her handsome eye.

And then one day, when she was picking around in the driveway she happened to find a cigarette that someone had tossed out from a car. It was still lit, and just in curiosity the hen put it in her beak and took a few puffs. She liked the taste and it made her feel quite rakish to be smoking, just as she had seen well-dressed ladies doing on the front porch. She held the cigarette gracefully in one claw, and tossed her head at a mischievous angle. She saw other hens in the yard looking at her with surprise, and caught a gleam of attention from the big red rooster. Suddenly she determined to have a gay life while it was still possible. Why should she spend all her time looking after the chickens?

The whole neighbourhood is still talking about the lively doings that followed. You would never have known she was the same hen. She had her feathers smartly shingled, she bought some new clothes, and very thin yellowish silk stockings, and she smoked all the time. She got herself a swift little roadster with a rumble seat behind, and she could be seen flashing along the North Shore roads at a great pace. She didn't even need to stop driving to light a cigarette: she bought a car that had an electric lighter. She never got home to the roost until late, for she usually dined out at some gay roadhouse. If her legs were tired now, it was from dancing. She even had a fifty-trip ticket on the railroad, and the only worry she had was to find places to park the car while she went to a matinée in town.

And while the gay hen was leading this exciting life, with a little blue trail of cigarette smoke behind her, where were the chickens? Why, they were in the field, as Blythe had noticed. They had wandered across the road and you could see them over there, scattered at their own sweet will. They were having a grand time I dare say, but they were getting their feet wet and eating all sorts of dangerous things. They got into poison ivy and they coughed at night. They were getting quite tough, and there is nothing more regrettable in a chicken.

One day the gay hen was on her way back from a tea party in Great Neck. She wanted to smoke a cigarette, but the lighter in her car had got out of order. So she stopped and waved to the first car that came along, to borrow a match.

It happened to be Mr. Mistletoe's car, Dean

Swift, with the whole family on board. Of course Mr. Mistletoe had a match, and hastened to give a light to such a smart-looking hen. Blythe, sitting in the back of the car, was greatly interested. She watched the hen carefully, and then began to sing her little ditty. "Chickens, chickens, in the field," she sang.

The gay hen was just tossing away the match with a debonair gesture. She was ready to step on the gas and go scooting off down the road to another party in Locust Valley. Suddenly she realized how tired she was of a roadhouse life. When she heard Blythe's song she thought with sadness of the chickens running wild all over the fields, not wearing rubbers, eating wrong food, quarrelling and using bad words, growing up rowdy and tough.

She threw away the cigarette, and drove home fast, very fast. She leaped out of the smart roadster and called all the chickens home from the field, with the old bedtime call that they still remembered. They were very big now, but once more she took them all under her wings as best she could, though they kicked and skirmished so that she was awake most of the night.

The next day she cleaned out the rumble seat,

which was full of cigarette ashes dropped by her dissipated friends. Now, when she goes driving, the rumble is full of chickens, enjoying the air. There isn't even room for a package of cigarettes on the front seat, because it's crowded with fresh vegetables, from the stalls along the roads near Farmingdale. . . .

And if the story has really been a success, and is told in a drowsy tone, to the rhyming hum of the car, Blythe is now asleep. She doesn't wake up until the Dean hits that bump at the bottom of the home driveway.

THE PEANUT WAGON

BLACKBERRIES reddened down by the pond; the pink hollyhocks were eight feet tall by the kitchen steps; the white phlox was out along the brick path; every afternoon the children's wet bathing suits hung on the line near the grape arbor. The sight of those bathing suits, and letters from Christopher describing the good time he was having at Camp near Port Jefferson, made the animals restless. It was midsummer, and they needed a change. Donny, after a specially alluring letter from Christopher describing how he had slept alone in the woods, made the suggestion, "Let's go camping," he said.

It was a grand idea. There was really no reason why they shouldn't go away for a little trip. The Grape Arbor Tea Room had made a good profit so they had some money to spend. The children would miss them, but a little separation would make them all appreciate each other better when they returned. And Mr. Mistletoe, who was trying to do some writing, was keen about the idea.

Donny was given the money and sent in town to buy what was needed for the expedition. He did not often go to the city, and when he did it was an excitement for the whole household. Fourchette scrubbed some food stains from his Palm Beach suit, and pressed it, and cleaned his Panama hat. Mr. Mistletoe gave him a bath with flea soap and trimmed his whiskers. Nothing could make hairy old Donny look like a real commuter: at his very best he looked more like a sailing-ship skipper togged out in unaccustomed shore clothes. His Panama hat had shrunk a bit and was too small for his big shaggy head. But at any rate he looked most respectable. The whole family lined up to inspect him, straightened his hat, put a dahlia in his button hole. Mr. Mistletoe lent him an old brief-case, to carry packages, and Donny went off very pleased with himself.

While Donny was in town that day an exciting thing happened. Fourchette was at the A. & P., buying provisions for the trip, when the Glen Cove peanut wagon came by. You've seen it trundling gently along the shore road drawn by a thoughtful white horse. It carries ice cream cones and candy and crackers and popcorn and ginger ale—all the things people have a hunger for on hot weather picnics. It has a sign on it that says FRESH ROSTED PEANUTS, and the steam-pipe of the peanut cooker comes up through the roof of the wagon and makes a merry sing-song whistling as the wagon rolls by. When Fourchette saw the wagon she was struck with a great idea. That would be just the thing for them to take their expedition in. She rushed out to ask George Vlachos, the peanut man, if he would sell his wagon.

George didn't like the idea of selling the wagon, but he said he would rent it to them for a while. This would give him a chance to go back to Greece for a holiday. The price came rather high, and Fourchette had to break open the kittens' banks and also Donny's china pig with a slit in its back. But she was convinced that in the lunch wagon they could combine business with pleasure. They could sell hot dogs and ice cream cones to the animals along the road. Animals love these things and rarely get them. She paid George Vlachos the rent at once, for fear he might change his mind, and drove him down to the station so he could get back to Glen Cove by train. Then she brought the wagon back to the house. Everyone was amazed.

The kittens wanted to drive the peanut wagon down to the station to meet Donny's train late that afternoon. But Escargot was very tactful. No, he said, don't do that, because Donny will come home very happy and excited and eager to tell us all about his day in town. It would be unkind to take the wind out of his sails by having such a Surprise waiting for him at the station. Let him tell us about his adventures first.

This was true thoughtfulness. They hid the peanut wagon in the garage and took the white horse (whose name was Bowser) into the back lot to enjoy some grass.

Donny came back on the 4.59 express, which is due at Roslyn at 5.46. He had had a great day. As a matter of fact he got through his errands very quickly, and in his elation at being relieved for a few hours of his home responsibilities he went to a movie. There he sat happily, watching the pictures and whining a little with applause. He did not mention this to the others, however, as somehow he thought it better to speak of the difficult shopping he had done and how hot and crowded New York was. He admitted that he had a frosted chocolate in a drugstore, but they had guessed that already because he forgot to wipe off some of the foam that stuck to his moustache. He was specially proud because he had met the fashionable Mr. Airedale in the Penn Station, and Mr. Airedale had invited him to ride in the club car among all the important people from Oyster Bay. Donny made himself quite at home in the club car, crossed one leg over another like a Prominent Commuter, and talked easily about just having run in to Town to buy a camping outfit. In fact, his behaviour had been so clever all day that no one in New York suspected him. The man at the soda fountain looked at him rather queerly, and said to himself "Isn't it odd how much some people look like dogs." But no one actually found him out.

The animals were delighted with the things he

had brought. There were little ponchos and fishing tackle for the kittens, a flashlight for Escargot, flannel shirts for the rabbits, and a pair of very becoming khaki knickers for Fourchette. He had not forgotten the remark she often made when they went on picnics, that knickers are really much more modest than a skirt.

When he had told them all his adventures, and taken off his good clothes, and had a roll on the gravel to express his satisfaction at being home again, Fourchette said: "And now we have something to show you." They took him behind the garage and explained the peanut wagon to him.

Donny was so tickled with the wagon that later in the evening he had one of those barking spells dogs sometimes get, when they go on and on, barking so wildly that they can't stop—although they have quite forgotten what they're barking about. It happens specially on hot still nights when there is a queer heavy silence in the air. He barked and barked until Mr. Mistletoe, already cross because there were so many moths fluttering under his desk lamp, rushed outdoors in his pyjamas, very angry. He chased Donny all round the garden in the moonlight, and sent him to bed. So a day of too much excitement ended, as it often does, with punishment.

* * * *

But the next day that was all forgotten. Fourchette was up early, stowing the provisions into the wagon. The peanut stove was lit and sent up its gay whistle into the warm blue morning. Bowser, the white horse, who had been a little lonely without his friend George Vlachos, now began to see that this new adventure would be good fun. He was given a big breakfast, and Perez even fried an egg for him, something Bowser had never tasted before. Hops and Malta each had a very small suitcase, to hold their toothbrushes and bathing suits and a few toys. Then they arranged themselves for the journey. Binny and Bunny wanted to do the selling, but everyone knew their hungry natures, and it was feared they would eat more than they would sell. Fourchette took charge of the business department, she lay comfortably on a shelf and kept watch on the stock. Escargot was near, high up on one of the glass windows of the wagon where he could see everything and Fourchette could ask him questions in arithmetic in case she got puzzled. Escargot's thoughtful mind was very quick at figures. The others climbed up into the broad front seat. Donny held the reins, the rabbits and kittens sat beside him, continually asking "How soon can I drive?"

Now they were ready, and Donny was panting with eagerness. All the children of the neighbourhood had gathered to see them start, Mr. Mistletoe had hoisted the flag on the pole. Blythe wept a little because she could not go too. Then with a wave from Mr. and Mrs. Mistletoe and a cheer from all the children and a broad grin from Perez, off they went.

Out from the green shadows of the Estates, out into the open sunshine of the big roads, went the peanut wagon. First they had some errands to do. They stopped at the post office to ask Mrs. Breen to hold their mail for them until they returned. They stopped at Mr. Hamilton's feed warehouse down by the railroad: Donny went into the cool grainy smell of that interesting place where so many sacks are piled up, and brought out a big bag of oats for Bowser. Fourchette, who looked very handsome in her khaki knickers and a red bandanna handkerchief knotted round her neck, visited Roulston's grocery for some chocolate-covered graham crackers as a treat for Donny. Then they rolled down the winding hill, past Mr. Pickering's curiosity shop, past what Helen calls the Muriel Building (she means *Memorial*). They halted at the bakery to get some bezluks and hodas. Bezluk and Hoda are really the names of the bakers, but the children had given those words to two very delicious kinds of buns they always got there when they were hungry after bathing. A *bezluk* is a soft bun with raisins in it, a *hoda* is a crunchier kind with sprinklings of brown sugar. As soon as the rabbits saw the bezluks and hodas they began to say they were hungry; but that was absurd, they weren't even out of the village yet.

They meant to take the turnpike, but Bowser started along the Shore Road by force of habit, and it didn't really matter. So they went past Cedarmere, and under the long arcade of trees by the Engineers' Club, and stopped to sell some of the fresh buns to the black swans at Glenwood. Everywhere the peanut whistle sang its shrill call, like the Pied Piper, and hungry animals came out to bark and wave and welcome them. They didn't get on very fast, there were too many customers, some of whom followed them far along the road. Fourchette was kept busy serving ice cream cones to cats, and hot frankfurters to dogs, and peanuts and popcorn to birds and squirrels who came down from the trees to see what was happening. Seagulls came slanting in from the harbour, and frogs gargled at them from the ponds. Such a crowd gathered when they stopped that they had to pull off to one side to avoid holding up the traffic. Bowser, who proved to be quite a character, always had some humorous comment to make about the cars that hurried past them. He did not even complain when birds and squirrels sat on his back while they ate their peanuts.

Willow trees were rumpled silver in the breeze, bright regiments of tiger lilies paraded on hillsides, the tide pressed high among the reeds and on sandy beaches, strong salty smells sharpened the dulcet air. The road was firm under their rolling wheels, under Bowser's ambling hooves. *I know a secret*, the little whistle seemed to shrill. Life goes down into the strong earth, life moves in the pushing tide, and life surrounded the wagon with beauty. The shining weather blessed them with colour and laughter in honour of their innocence. For animals are cruel but not cowardly, they are fierce but not mean, they do mischief but never malice. They make no plans, they have no hopes, they ask no questions. Because they are so happy, human beings labour to support them. Their meals are waiting, their needs supplied, men are the humble gods who tend them. As electricity is the servant of man, so is man the servant of animals. Their lack of malice makes them our conquerors. *I know a secret!* shrilled the little whistle: *Life is its own reward.*

* * * *

As they had taken such a roundabout road they could not reach Lloyds Neck that day. They spent the afternoon peacefully dawdling on the winding ways past Dosoris, Lattingtown, Locust Valley—a region of great estates where they found few customers. Bowser, who knows all the geography of Nassau County, told them that the name Dosoris comes from *Dos Uxoris*, which is Latin and means the Dowry of the Wife. But evidently it was just a phrase he had been told, for when they questioned him he could not say whose wife it was or what was a dowry.

Donny said that a dowry was a kind of rowboat, but Fourchette, always a very modern cat and full of decided views, contradicted him. A dowry, she said, is the property a woman gives to any husband who is kind enough to marry her. It is an old exploded idea, a relic of the dark ages, she said quite fiercely. "When I married that lazy loafing cat from the A. & P. I had a can of Norwegian sardines as a dowry. I thought it was safe, for the key to open it had been lost; but within a week he had got a plumber to open it for him and ate them all. That was the beginning of the end. If Malta ever marries, I hope it will be some honest ambitious cat who is willing to work for her."

"However, I regret nothing," she added, embracing the kittens fondly.

Talking cheerfully about this and that, they reached the popular beach at Bayville. Here a curious incident happened, which had much effect on their affairs later. Among the crowd of animals that surrounded them was a dark wizened monkey who belonged to a hand-organ man. The monkey was very thirsty, he had put in a hard long day collecting pennies, and they gave him an ice cream cone. The kittens were enchanted with him: he wore a red jacket and trousers and a very tiny doughboy cap, all extremely dirty. He had a habit of taking off his cap with a quick gesture whenever anything was said to him, and holding out a small dark hand. His forehead was very wrinkled and he seemed nervous and tired.

They unhitched Bowser and left the wagon on the beach while they went for a bathe. The keeper of the bathing pavilion made some protest about Bowser going in. There was no bath-house big enough for him, and also he had no bathing suit.

"How ridiculous!" said Donny angrily. "Bathing suits are absurd anyhow, a relic of the dark ages—like dowries," he added, for he was always quick to pick up a new word.

The keeper was impressed, for he did not know what dowries were either, but he said it was the rule. They hired a dozen bathing suits, at a special rate, and pinned them all together to make a kind of cloak for Bowser.

Escargot, on account of his shell. was allowed to go in as he was.

While they were in the water they heard a sort of commotion on the beach, but they paid no attention, thinking it was just the natural admiration of the people at Bowser's unusual bathing costume. They had to wait quite a while for Escargot to come back from the water, but at last they started off again. When they were well on the road a dark wrinkled face suddenly popped up from the sack of unroasted peanuts. It was the monkey. Weary of his difficult life as a hand-organist he had come along as a stowaway. He had burrowed into the sack of peanuts and hidden there.

"Oh, then that was what all the noise was about?" said Fourchette.

"Yes," said the monkey. "It was very comic. I could hear it all. Tonio—that's the organ-man—was furious at the bath-house keeper. Tonio said I'd been stolen, and how could he find me again with such a crowd on the beach. The keeper said it was none of *his* business, and Tonio threatened to take one of the bath-house keeper's children as a substitute."

They were glad to have the monkey join them, as he was an amusing companion, though Fourchette was horrified at the condition of his clothes and would not let the kittens sit next to him, which caused some bickering. They christened him Dosoris as he was an unexpected addition to their resources.

It was almost dark when they reached the old town of Oyster Bay. There was a good deal of traffic in the streets and they had some difficulty in finding a place to park. They were moved on several times by policemen who said they were causing a nuisance. Donny saw some of the prominent people with whom he had ridden in the club car, and barked gaily to them, but none of them recognized him. Finally they drove on through the town to the cemetery. They left the wagon under a tree and went up to Theodore Roosevelt's grave, where they felt sure they would not be turned away. They all lay down respectfully outside the railings of the grave and slept in peace. Fourchette was afraid that this might be thought a liberty, but Donny replied that T. R. was always interested in animals and would not mind. I think myself that no nicer tribute was ever paid him.

* * * *

It was the next afternoon when they finally got to Lloyds Neck. Escargot and the rabbits had been raised to such a pitch of expectancy by Donny's praise of that country that nothing could have surprised them. But no one is ever disappointed in Lloyds Neck. When Bowser, trotting merrily, pulled the wagon out onto the long narrow strip that joins the Neck to the mainland, they were all thrilled by the view. Escargot stretched his short-sighted eyes to their very longest, like telescopes, to see as much as possible. Even Dosoris, who had spent most of his life in towns and liked crowded places where pennies were frequent, was much impressed by the scenery. The water was going out, and the quiet inlet of Lloyd Harbour had that fine savoury low-tide smell that gives you such an appetite. The rabbits kept exclaiming with hunger, and wanted the wagon to stop every few yards to let them try some of the green things they saw. But they pushed on, along the shore, past the beautiful old Colonial manor, through woods and blue glimpses, until they came to the big tree. There they turned in on a lumber trail. The black dog who is chained up at the farmhouse kept shouting wildly "Private Property! Private Property!" but a couple of frankfurters stopped that.

There was some hard pulling for Bowser, up sandy slopes, but once over the crest of the hill they went easily down through the woods toward the Sound. Donny had picked out the perfect place for a camp. There is a little cliff that overlooks the water, where a circle of trees surrounds a grassy clearing. The beach is rocky, but there are patches of sand, and in late afternoon light the water shines with a marvellous golden-green clearness. Bushes of sweet-fern give off a warm fragrance, and there is any amount of driftwood for building fires. They did not need to bother about a tent, for there was room for them all to sleep under the wagon, except Bowser, who made himself comfortable in a sheltered little grove of cedars not far away.

Fourchette, who always liked everything neat and orderly, said that the first thing to do was to wash Dosoris's clothes. They had some difficulty in persuading him to take them off: he had worn the red jacket and pantaloons, and the doughboy cap, so long, that he really believed they were part of himself. Also, he did not seem to know much about water and how comfortable it is to splash about in. He made a great fuss, but finally they got him undressed and forced him into the water, while Fourchette gave the clothes a good scrub and hung them on a tree to air. Like so many people who make a fuss about doing something, once he was in that warm green bathing he became enthusiastic. Also he quite refused to put on the clothes again, he was so much more comfortable without them. He did not give up the cap, which he was proud of, and continued to take it off hastily every time anyone spoke to him, but the red jacket and trousers were left hanging on the tree.

Meanwhile the kittens had been fishing, from a large rock near the shore, and Escargot had found some snails he could talk to. The long twilight softened around them, and the watchful Fourchette began to observe signs of peevishness—both in herself and the others. After two days on the road they were all tired, and also they had been eating too many sweets. Even the rabbits, usually so gentle, were complaining that they could find no plantain in the woods. As they gathered for supper Escargot just escaped being trodden upon by Bowser, and asked him sharply to be more careful. Dosoris was rather annoyed by repeated references to fleas, and made some brisk retorts to Donny. Then they discovered they had forgotten to bring any water and had nothing to drink but ginger ale and sarsaparilla, which Bowser did not care for. The best thing to do was to go to bed, and they did so. Escargot slept with his flashlight lighted beside him, so that no one would walk on him in the dark.

A LETTER FROM FOURCHETTE

WE DO not know all the adventures that the animals had while camping, but we have a glimpse of their activities in a letter that Fourchette wrote to Louise. When the peanut wagon left, Louise gave Fourchette a fountain pen filled with ink, and Helen gave her a tablet of paper, and they asked her to write. Some time went by without any news, but at last a letter came. Fourchette was a good writer: as you will notice, she made only twelve mistakes in spelling in a very long letter. And one of those we must excuse, as she copied it from the peanut wagon.

This was the letter:—

Grape Arbor Camp
Lloyds Neck, L. I.

DEAR LOUISE AND HELEN:—

I am sorry I did not write before, but if you ever go camping you will understand how much there is to do. Something happening every moment. But this afternoon Donny and Bowser are going to Huntington to get supplies and can mail a letter. I have sent Hops and Malta down the beach to go fishing, and the rabbits with them to keep them out of mischeif. Fortunately the rabbits are of a cautious and sencible disposition, they are as good as two nursemaids. I have given them the job of seeing that the kittens clean their teeth every morning, though Hops and Malta do not like doing it in salt water. We have to be careful of our fresh water, as it all has to be brought from the farmhouse on the other side of the Neck. Donny started to dig a well, but it is a much bigger job than digging for moles, and he gave up.

The monkey we picked up on the road, Dosoris by name, is a great problem to me. Really sometimes I get disscouraged, raising a family is no end of toil. I get so fidgety I just have to skin up a tree to cool off. Dosoris is always in some pickle or other and seems never to have had any real home training. The first day or so he was quite ill from eating to many peanuts, then he recovered and became very mischeivious but he is so comic in his ways he keeps us bawling with laughter. The other day a cock pheasant came to call on us, a beautiful golden bird (very good eating, they tell me) with feathers coloured like a whole box of new crayons, yellow and red and blue and green, how you would have liked to see him. He came over from the big Marshall Field estate near here and was rather proud. Very high-hat, the kittens called him, where they pick up their slang I don't know. Dosoris took off his little cap to him, the way he does to everybody, and held out his hand, it's a habit from being always in the organ buisness, but the pheasant thought Dosoris was making fun of him and became very haughty. Well, we were all flattered to have a visit from such a handsome party, I wished you could see Donny's eyes stick out, he did not know there were such handsome birds in the world. It was all he could do to mind his manners when the visitor came strutting up. I gave him the Emergency signal just in time. We gave the pheasant some popcorn and everything was going nicely when Dosoris sneaked up behind and pulled out three of his grand golden feathers.

The pheasant was furious and I don't blame him. Of course Dosoris was up a tree in an instant, grinning and chattering and taking off his cap in his irritating way. He stuck the feathers in his cap and was delighted with his mischeif. The pheasant went off very angry, saying he would report the matter to Mr. Marshall Field, so we have been a bit nervous. But we hope the pheasant would not dare say anything to Mr. Field because he had no buisness going off the Field estate. Where we are of course is Private Property.

That brings me to another adventure. It happened, as things always do, when we were not at all prepared for visitors. Escargot spends most of his time down by the water, he is happy to get a chance to go bathing again, he says it reminds him of Normandy. Perhaps he was a bit careless, anyhow while he was idling on a wet rock a seagull spied him, and astonished at the sight of such a large lucious snail made a swoop at him and in fact seized him. We were all horribly dismayed and I thought all was over, but we shouted such screams of anger that the gull was startled and dropped him. Escargot was badly frightened, and for a long time we could not persuade him to come out of his shell so we could not tell if he was hurt or not. At last he did so, very pale. He was only bruised, but nervous. While we were all upset by this accident and were ministering to the troubled snail we were horrified to see a man approaching.

We were alarmed, we feared it was someone to move us off this happy spot which we have made so much our own. Also we were not pleased at the idea of any grown-up person intruding upon us, specially at a moment of suffering. Escargot again retreated into his privacy and Dosoris kept taking off his cap and gesticulating for a penny. It was queer to see how the presence of a human being again brought out all that monkey's worst manners, after we thought we had dissiplined him into some sensible behaviour.

The stranger was surprised to see us there, but I must say he was a friendly man. He gave Dosoris a penny, and explained that he had seen the monkey's clothes (still hanging on a tree) and thought them some kind of flag or signal. He knew how to behave with animals, for he sat down quietly and we soon got used to him. Donny gave him a good smelling and believed him to be all right. There was still a good deal of surprise in his looks, but he bought some rosted peanuts and we had a talk. He told us that he and some other people had bought all this piece of land, and he was very enthusiastic about the improvements they were going to make. There would be big concrete roads all through here, and electric light, and laid out in building lots. Why, he said, when this gets developed it will be worth twenty-five hundred an acre. How would you like to buy a couple of lots?

I think he was a little ashamed to have mentioned money, because right away Dosoris held out his hand.

Donny admitted he had always wanted to buy a few acres of land near the water, to retire to when the Roslyn Estates get civilized, but we all protested against this idea of developing Lloyds Neck with real estate schemes. But this man was a good salesman, he got out maps and more than once I was afraid he would have Donny signed up to buy something we could not possibly afford. Besides, why should we buy the property when we were using it anyway free of charge.

The man stayed to supper with us. It was a still evening and he lit a fire on the beach to keep away the mosquitoes, although he said there weren't any. We told stories for the kittens before they went to bed, and the visitor enjoyed them highly. He said that real estate men were always fond of fairy tales, and told us some of his own, about building houses on the South Shore of Long Island. Then he made a suggestion that excited us very much.

My family are all good talkers, he said, and I have a brother who is a Radio Announcer at station M.E.O.W. Those stories of yours are so good, he said, you ought to broadcast them. I know my brother would like to get you to tell some of them into the mike. Grown-up people like to hear stories before they go to bed, it takes their minds off anything disagreeable they have been doing to each other during the day. My brother would get you some money for broadcasting your stories, and then you could afford to buy some of this property.

Isn't that a wonderful idea? We are all greatly thrilled about it.

When he left he was very kind. He told us to go ahead and use this place as if it was our own. He said that would be the finest kind of advertisement for the whole property, and that he would save this special corner of beach for the Grape Arbor Camp.

Well, Louise and Helen, this is the longest letter I ever wrote, but you will be glad to hear we are having such a good time. We will be home soon. I hope you are all good children, no screeching, and that no one has had to sit on the Church Bench.

Your loving cat,
FOURCHETTE.

There is one thing in Fourchette's letter that needs to be explained. Once Mr. Mistletoe bought an old yellow bench from Mr. Zeifman's antique store down by the Mill Pond. He painted it white and put it in the garden, where it was much admired. And indeed it had a graceful simple shape that was very lovely. Mr. Zeifman said it came from an old church in Huntington, which had sold its picturesque old benches and put in pews. This bench, having lived long years in a church, was supposed to give peaceful thoughts to people who sat on it. So when anyone screeched or squabbled or got savage at croquet, he was supposed to go and sit on the Church Bench until he got Good Ideas.

STORY OF THE THRUSH'S NEST

THE story that most impressed the Real Estate Man, that evening at Lloyds Neck, was the one about the Thrush's Nest. It was first told by Mr. Mistletoe when they invited him out to the Grape Arbor Tea Room, and all the animals knew that it was perfectly true. It would be a good thing if all Real Estate Men would read this story, because it tells what happens to people who live in houses that are too big for them and too expensive to keep up.

The thrush lived near Mr. Mistletoe's lawn. As we have said before, *lawn* is too smooth a word. That was the spring all the workmen were there, and a spread of grass constantly trafficked over by ten children (four Mistletoes and half a dozen neighbours) and any number of dogs, plumbers, ash men, masons, carpenters and cesspool drainers, washed out by Long Island thunderstorms and sliced into divots by croquet mallets, is likely to be a little untidy. And so it was. Mr. Mistletoe tried hard, but his face had a discouraged look. Almost any fine evening towards katydid time you could see him out there, picking up pebbles Blythe had thrown for the kittens to chase, or bones that Donny had discarded, or looking for the croquet hoop.

But the thrush didn't mind all this. She even seemed to admire the place, and that spring the weather was so moist that there were plenty of worms. A worm means to a thrush much what a hot frankfurter means to a hungry child on a picnic—except that to her it looks like a hot dog five or six feet long.

At one side of his garden Mr. Mistletoe had put up a deck tennis court. Deck tennis is a kind of miniature tennis they play on board ship, not with rackets and a ball but by throwing and catching a rubber quoit which is tossed across the net. The rules and scoring are just like tennis, and the court is like a tennis court but smaller. Mr. Mistletoe had marked it out very carefully with narrow white tape neatly held down by staples. But in one place this tape had got broken, so there was a loose end.

It was the time of year when birds are building nests. The thrush had just picked out a good site for hers, in the big oak tree above the drive, and then that loose white end of tape caught her eye. So while Mr. Mistletoe was loitering about the garden with nothing particular to do—and that was unusual, for people with four children generally have something definite to do, and someone to whom it ought to be done—he saw the thrush tugging fiercely at the piece of tape. There was something really very comic about the violence of her efforts. She braced her feet and jerked as hard as possible, many times in quick succession. But it wouldn't come. She would pause, pant a little, and you could see her speckled bosom heave. She was a stout matronly thrush, probably not as flexible as she had been once. You could almost hear her say to herself, "Well, for goodness sake!" when the tape wouldn't budge. Then she would try again. She did not know about the staples Mr. Mistletoe had so carefully hammered into the ground.

Mr. Mistletoe and the whole family admired

her from a distance. She was so much in earnest that it seemed a pity to disappoint her. Mr. Mistletoe sent Christopher indoors for the big pair of scissors. They cut off the loose end, and then kept away at a polite distance. Sure enough, the thrush flew down from the tree where she had been watching, seized the ribbon, and flew off, so much excited, she forgot to say Thank you. And a few moments later, there she was again, hauling at the rest of the tape as hard as ever.

Perhaps it was generous of Mr. Mistletoe, or perhaps it was merely silly, but to see how much tape the thrush would use he sacrificed his whole deck tennis court. He hasn't played deck tennis since. There must have been two hundred feet of tape, but they cut it all up into pieces and she took every bit. It was a great afternoon for her. She must have thought she had found a tape-mine. So that the stout thrush wouldn't even have to stoop, Mr. Mistletoe hung all the tapes on the Nervous Prostration wire that runs between two trees. She flew busily to and fro, carrying the streamers to the oak tree on the other side of the house.

The kittens, of course, knew about the Nervous

Prostration wire, but the Real Estate Man, when Fourchette told this story, asked what it was.

The Nervous Prostration wire was a relic of the time when Donny was not well and had such a spell of peevishness. He growled so much, and made himself so disagreeable to delivery men and visitors, and seemed to have such an appetite for trousers, that everyone got worried about him. They took him over to see a doctor who runs a boarding house for dogs in Sea Cliff, and the doctor felt his pulses. (A dog has four pulses, one in each leg, and he felt them all.) Then the doctor looked at his eyes and his tongue and talked to him, and finally he asked about the conditions of Donny's home life.

Mr. Mistletoe attempted to describe the conditions of Donny's life, as well as one can ever describe such delicate matters to a stranger. He told the doctor about the children, and how Donny's time was spent, and finally the doctor said: "This dog has a kind of nervous prostration. He's not as young as he was, and your children are evidently too lively for him. They tire him out."

Mr. Mistletoe thought that that was quite possible, and said he had sometimes felt that way himself.

"You must see that Donny gets more quiet," said the doctor. "He ought to take a bromide tablet every day, and he must have a quiet nap after lunch. It would be a good thing to keep him chained up part of the time, in a shady place, so he won't be always on the go. Put a wire between two trees, so his chain can slide along it, that will give him room to move about a bit."

The wire was put there, and was known as the Nervous Prostration wire. Donny used to brag about all this a good deal, and sometimes I believe Mr. Mistletoe envied him when he saw him resting in the shade. Donny soon got better, and the wire was no longer used.

But this story is about the thrush. As we were saying, she took every bit of tape. She used it to build a nest that was a source of scandal to all the other birds. It was almost as big as a beehive, very disorderly and pretentious. Even Abe Blackbird, the lawyer, who rarely meddled in other people's affairs, warned her against making a nest of that sort. But she had been so puffed up with ambition that she was determined to have the biggest and most prominent home in the Roslyn Estates. She even persuaded a photographer to come and make a picture post-card of it, as they do of the handsomer houses.

During the time that she was raising her children Mr. Mistletoe was abroad, so he never knew how they got on. Mr. and Mrs. Mistletoe, after watching Donny taking it easy under the trees, decided that they also deserved a holiday. For if the children could give a big sheep dog Nervous Prostration, you can imagine what they could do to their parents. And when Mr. and Mrs. Mistletoe came home again, as soon as they had counted up the children and made sure that everything was all right, they asked about the thrush's nest. There was sad news to be told. The big nest had not been a success. It was draughty, inconvenient, and insecure. In the August thunderstorm season the whole untidy bundle had blown away in ruin and wreck. The young thrushes had been cast upon the world, and the stout matronly thrush was working somewhere as a stenographer.

It is a sad story and a true one, and as Mr. Mistletoe always added, it was his own fault. He should have let that stout thrush take only a few strips of tape, not the whole thing at once.

Of course she was a little bit crazed with the sentimental excitement of the nesting season, and he should have protected her against her own folly. Perhaps the same thing is true in building a mind. A mind is only a little nest in the infinite oak-tree of life; but it needs to be comfortable and secure, a place where you can hatch eggs of thought; and it must be strong enough not to be blown away in sudden thunder-squalls. Education, I suppose, is like that tape. You can't pull it out of the ground unless some one loosens it for you, but the good parent or teacher will parcel it out gradually in convenient shreds. He won't chop up too much of it at once.

And education differs from that tape in one very important way. There's no end to it.

GISSING AND THE TELEPHONE

ONE of the best amusements for a winter evening, when it gets dark early, is the Magic Lantern. Its real name, I believe, is a Post Card projector; but Magic Lantern sounds better. You fasten the wire to any electric light socket, and put photographs or post cards or pictures cut from magazines into the lantern. It shows them, much enlarged and bright and clear in all their colours, on the screen (which you hang on the dining-room double doors). All interesting post cards are carefully saved for the Lantern: you wouldn't believe what a collection we have. The German cards are specially lovely: the series illustrating the adventures of Hansel and Gretel are great favourites. You get Christopher to tell the story aloud and Mr. Mistletoe throws the pictures on the screen at the proper moment. The floor is thick with little girls, so (the room being dark) you have to be careful where you step. Our neighbourhood is fertile in small girls, and they make good audiences. They deserve encouragement, for some day they will grow up into Women's Clubs and pay people real money to come and give them lectures.

Even better than the post cards are the pictures you make yourself. If it's a wet afternoon you can set the children to work with cardboard, pencils, and paints or crayons, and let them make drawings of their own to be shown in the lantern. There is a fine thrill in seeing your own work displayed in that way. The pictures must be of the right size to fit into the lantern, and of course any lettering on them has to be done backwards so it will come out correct on the screen. Mr. Mistletoe greatly enjoys doing lantern pictures. His kind of art, which is crude but strong, is highly relished by that intelligent audience. Home-made fairy tales deserve home-made illustrations. Some of those pictures have done service for years and are welcomed again with fresh admiration every winter when the Lantern Season begins at Hallowe'en. I am greatly tempted to put in here one of Mr. Mistletoe's works of art so that you can see an actual picture the children have so often praised.

If you won't make fun of it I think I will; and tell you the story that goes with it. It is a story about the dog called Gissing, when he was very young. He was only a puppy and knew very little.

In the house where Gissing lived there was a speaking tube in the hall upstairs. This speaking tube was a great joy. When children blew in it it made a loud whistling squeal down in the kitchen. Done suddenly it often startled cooks and cats half out of their wits. It sounded like the squeak of a mouse as big as a police dog. But like many amusing jokes this got overdone. And so, to prevent the speaking tube becoming a nuisance, it was agreed that it was a private magic telephone to Santa Claus and must not be used except in the week before Christmas. Santa Claus, like everyone else, does not care to be bothered with unnecessary telephone calls. Like many other wise people he does not allow his number to be listed in the book, and only tells it to his intimate friends.

But of course in the week before Christmas everyone is so busy that a little extra squeaking in the kitchen does not matter.

Now Gissing, arriving in the house as a very small puppy, heard so much about this Santa Claus telephone that he really believed it. He heard the children making their plans, and writing out lists, and then blowing in the mouthpiece until it squawked and announcing down the tube their desires for Christmas. He wished very much that he too could telephone to Santa Claus and tell what he wanted. But he felt bashful about doing it, and a little ashamed because he did not understand very well just what Christmas was. He heard all the children talking about it, and he tried to pick up some information by listening, but he did not learn anything definite. You know how it is: when everyone else seems to know about something that you yourself don't understand, you don't like to admit your ignorance. You listen carefully, hoping you'll overhear some remark that will explain what it's all about.

Gissing spoke in a casual way to the others,

hoping to lead them into saying something that would help him to know what was going to happen. He would say "Christmas will be fun, won't it!" or some such innocent thing. But their replies, though enthusiastic, did not help much. In his heart he was lonely because he felt there was some great secret that they knew and he didn't. "Oh, I wish someone would tell me what Christmas is," he said to himself. "Is it something to eat? Is it something to wear? Is it a game? Is it a person? And who is this mysterious Santa Claus?"

One day so much happened that Gissing felt more sure than ever that Christmas was going to be something very important. It was even a little frightening. From early morning the house was full of movement and hullabaloo. Tin horns were blown, there was crackling of paper parcels being unwrapped, and the living room was so crowded with children playing with new toys that he retired under the dining-room table. Even there he was not safe, for by chance he squatted on the electric bell, and after many visits had been made to the front door he was found and moved off. There were smells of balsam and evergreen, and a whiff of brandy from the kitchen. Most alarming of all, the pudding caught fire and was carried in blazing. It was all rather puzzling to a puppy, and Gissing lay under the couch feeling wistful. Everyone seemed too occupied to play with him, and he began to think that it was all because he had never talked into the magic telephone

After supper things quieted down a bit. The children were got to bed early. The grown-ups, exhausted by picking up so much paper and string, sat down to rest. Gissing saw his chance. With great labour he pulled his toy-box into the upstairs hall and stood on it so he could reach the speaking tube. He blew into it, and heard it squeal at the other end. Then he said, just as he had heard the children do, "Give me North Pole 1." To his great surprise he heard a deep voice coming back to him through the tube. "Santa Claus speaking," it said

Now we must refer to the picture, in which Mr. Mistletoe illustrated the scene with so much skill. You will see young Gissing standing on his toy-box, talking into the speaking tube. And you will see that the wire really did go all the way to Santa Claus's telephone at the North Pole.

Santa Claus had had a long day. He had just

got home, very tired after delivering toys all over the world. He was so tired that even before putting away the sleigh and the reindeer he had come into his house to sit down a few moments

Gissing Telephones to Santa Claus

and smoke a pipe. Everything was ready for a quiet evening. His slippers were warming in front of the fire; on the mantel a thermos jug of hot cocoa was waiting for him. He had left the door open to remind himself that he still had to go out and stable the reindeer for the night. You can see his footprints in the snow. You can even see the North Pole itself, which is striped red white and blue like a barber's pole.

(Of course in the picture done by Mr. Mistletoe for the Magic Lantern, all the colours are put in. I don't know whether the printer can copy all those beautiful colours. If he can't, and decides to print the picture in black and white, then my advice to you is to get out your paint-box and colour the picture yourself.)

You will also notice that the writing in the picture is carefully done backwards, so it would come out forwards on the screen. That is part of the Lantern's magic.

Santa was a little annoyed when the telephone rang. He believed that he had earned his ease. He was intending to rest his feet a bit, and then, with a happy feeling, he was going to tear off the 25 on the calendar pad that hung on the wall.

"Who is it?" he asked

"This is Gissing," said a small and rather frightened voice that sounded very far away. "You know, Gissing in the Roslyn Estates. At Mr. Mistletoe's house."

Of course Santa knew about the Roslyn Estates, but he had never heard of Gissing, who was still so young that his name had not been entered on the lists. Santa gets the names and addresses of all the dogs from the Town Hall in Manhasset, where the dog licenses are registered. However, he answered very kindly.

"Yes, Gissing," he said. "How are you?"

"Why, I'm fine," said Gissing, "but I thought I'd better tell you what I want for Christmas."

It was on the tip of Santa's tongue to say, a little crossly, "But Christmas is over. You're too late." But he could guess from the trembly sound of Gissing's voice that there must be some misunderstanding.

"All right, Gissing," he said in an encouraging voice. "What is it?"

"What have you got?" asked Gissing eagerly.

Santa Claus almost laughed. Gissing, even when he was a small puppy, was always rather impudent. Santa looked at his shelves. There were only a few toys remaining, now that all that year's Christmas presents had been delivered. You can see in the picture just what was left.

"Well," said Santa patiently, "I have a toy

schooner, a train, a doll, a rubber ball, a rake, a pail and shovel, a football, a white china cat, a paint-box, and a toy automobile."

Gissing was so excited he could hardly hold all those ideas in his head.

"Would you mind, please, repeating the list?" he asked politely.

Santa repeated, smiling to himself.

"I think I would like a white china cat," said Gissing. He wanted very much to ask for the toy aunbile also, but he restrained himself.

Santa Claus sighed at the thought of going all the way back to the Roslyn Estates that night. He was rather angry at Mr. Mistletoe for not having properly instructed Gissing about Christmas and told him the date. But he did not want anyone to be disappointed.

"Very well," he said. "You hang up your stocking, and the cat will be there in the morning. Merry Christmas!"

"Here's looking at you," replied Gissing. It was a phrase he had heard grown-ups say, and it was the only thing he could think of at the moment. He pulled his toy-box back into the nursery, quietly, so that no one would know what he had been up to, got out his largest stocking, and went to bed.

Santa Claus had a cup of hot cocoa, and gave some to the reindeer, who was peevish at having to go out again. But with such a light load to carry, the sleigh sped swiftly. Across the snowy curve of the world the red sleigh went flashing. Great gauzes of daffodil-yellow rippled and flickered in the blue dark, the wonderful Northern Lights. A brilliant star burned steadily right above the Pole—the North Star, the true Christmas Star. You can easily find it in the sky (unless you live South of the Equator) because the two stars in the end of the Dipper point straight to it.

It was the quietest night of the year, the night when all the children go to sleep at once because they are tired out with toys and excitements. Santa and the reindeer soon got over their irritation at having to go out again. It was very peaceful, even better than the hurry of Christmas Eve.

When Gissing woke up the next morning, there was the china cat. And not only the cat. Because Gissing's request had been so modest, Santa had brought along all the toys that were left—the schooner, the train, the doll, the ball, the rake, the pail and shovel, the football, the paint-box, and the aunbile.

It wasn't until Gissing was much older that he learned that Santa Claus had made a special trip, all the way from the North Pole to the Roslyn Estates. And that was why Gissing himself, when he grew up and went on a long adventure, was careful to get home on Christmas Eve, so that his puppies wouldn't be disappointed.

HOW THIS BOOK GOT PUBLISHED

WHEN the pleasure of mowing the lawn is past, then comes the pleasure of raking leaves. No wonder Helen is proud of having her birthday at the end of September, for perhaps autumn days are loveliest of all. The fields are yellow with goldenrod and blue with asters. The poison ivy runs up the trunks of the locust trees like a red and yellow flame. The air smells sweet of bonfires, and all kinds of smoky fragrance. Down in his greenhouses Mr. Steiger is burning tobacco to kill the chrysanthemum lice.

The time would soon come when the peanut wagon must be returned to George Vlachos. Even after they came back from camp the animals wanted to have as many expeditions in it as possible. Sometimes they took the children too, and all came home singing. The wagon was at its most picturesque plodding in the dusk up the long hill from the Village. Past the Clock Tower, and the house where George Washington had breakfast, it would roll steadily up the winding slope. Bowser refused to be hurried on that hill, and even those terribly big busses marked GLEN COVE EXPRESS had to take their time behind him. They would groan and grumble in all their gears, but Bowser insisted—and quite rightly—on his fair share of the road. A red lantern hung inside the wagon and cast a glow over all the company. There was a pink tinge in the little trail of steam floating from the peanut whistle.

But on this last expedition there were no children with them. The children were at school when the animals started before lunch. It was just as well, for this trip resulted in the greatest adventure of all, and it was good to have it a surprise.

They wanted to visit the Jericho Cider Mill, which always opens the first of October. Donny had inherited from Mr. Mistletoe a great passion for cider, particuarly when it was new and sweet. Every autumn the first visit to the Jericho mill was an Event. There is a little bar built outside the mill, and the glass jugs of bright golden juice stand sparkling in the sunshine. Mr. Tappen, who runs the mill since old Mr. Hicks retired, gives away glasses of cider free to everybody who buys a jug. It is said that people who drink largely of the Jericho cider will live to a great and happy age, and it seems to be true. Perhaps that is because it is made of honest old Quaker apples. Certainly there is a Quaker influence in the Jericho cider; after two glasses of it people always say *thee* to each other, instead of *you*, in the old Quaker fashion.

The animals were the first visitors to the mill that autumn, and when the peanut wagon halted beside the bar Mr. Tappen welcomed them gladly. No one else was there, so the smaller animals got out and sat on top of the counter, while Donny stood with his feet on the old brass rail just as he had seen Mr. Mistletoe do. Mr. Tappen served Bowser's cider in a pail, and they were all happy. The sun was warm and clear and a few toping flies were drinking greedily from puddles of spilled cider.

"Does thee remember the poem?" said Donny to Mr. Tappen, and repeated the following lines:

"So when the deep disgust takes hold
　　And I am dumb and dry,
I'll quit the folk who pester me
　　And tell the world good-by
And settle at the cider mill
　　In Jericho, L. I."

"What is that from?" asked Escargot.

"Doesn't thee know?" said Fourchette. "It's a verse from a poem Mr. Mistletoe wrote about this cider mill. He wrote it and got it printed in a book."

"No, thee never told me," said Escargot. He liked saying *thee*, because it was just like the French way of saying *tu* when you know people very well.

It may have been partly the cheerful influence of the clear autumn elixir they were drinking, for it was then that the great idea came to them. Escargot said it first.

"Look here," he said. "Thee told me about a big printing press not far from Roslyn. Instead of thee going to Station M. E. O. W. to broadcast our stories, the way thee is planning to do, why don't we write them out and take them over to that printing place? They're Long Island stories, and a Long Island publisher might like them."

They were amazed at the simplicity of this excellent thought.

"Very true," said Fourchette. "A book would be much better than just talking them on the air, because we'd have something to show for it."

"A book with pictures?" shouted Hops and Malta.

"My picture in it too!" squeaked Dosoris.

"Mr. Mistletoe would give us an introduction to Mr. Doubleday," said Donny.

"Think of the labour of writing them all out," said the rabbits. "Writing stories is hard work, see how much fuss Mr. Mistletoe makes about it."

"But Mr. Doubleday would pay us for it," said Escargot.

"It's a wonderful idea," said Donny. "We must think about it carefully."

Escargot had been sipping steadily at the magical cider, which reminded him of his own Normandy, a great cider country. His eyes were long and bright with enthusiasm. "Don't let's think about it," he said. "Let's do it. Let's go there right away and see what Mr. Doubleday says."

"I know where he works," said Bowzer. "It's in that big building over at Garden City. George Vlachos often went there about noon-time to sell things to the printers. They must work very hard because they are terribly hungry when they come out for their lunch hour. I don't know which one is Mr. Doubleday, but they all come out from the press room with ink on their hands."

They consulted Mr. Tappen who thought it a fine idea.

"If you hurry, you can get there before he closes for the afternoon," he said. So they had one last drink of cider all round, to wish luck to the venture. Then they set off along the Jericho Pike.

They were more nervous when they finally got to the Country Life Press. The peanut wagon drove into the circular driveway in front of the building, and they were startled at the size of the establishment. Beyond a blaze of autumn flowers they could see the printing machines flapping great white sheets of paper at them in a threatening way. Now they began to argue which one had better go in to see Mr. Doubleday, and all felt rather timid except Dosoris. He was eager to rush in, and insisted that he could finish the affair in no time. But they were certain that Dosoris was not the best person. His habit of whipping off his cap and holding out an appealing palm might make a bad impression. "A publisher sees quite enough of that sort of thing," said Fourchette.

It was decided that Escargot, who had made the suggestion, should be their representative. Escargot's quiet dignity and his slow thoughtful ways would be appreciated by Mr. Doubleday.

The kittens were impatient. "Hurry, hurry up!" Hops exclaimed. "He will stop work for the day and you'll be too late."

"Thee hold thy tongue," replied Escargot calmly.

The prudent snail was not to be hustled. He tucked a small bag of peanuts inside his shell, as a present for Mr. Doubleday. At his own pace, and pausing to admire the flower garden, he proceeded along the brick path and up the steps. Fortunately someone came out just then and held the front door open for him. He climbed the stairs perseveringly, and a pleasant young woman at a desk in the hall, noticing him on the floor, asked if she could do anything for him.

"I wish to see Mr. Doubleday," he said, outwardly bold but rather shaky deep inside his curly shell.

"Which Mr. Doubleday?" she asked, and this perplexed him for a moment; but he made the proper reply. "There is only one Mr. Doubleday," he said firmly.

He was escorted into a large library where he waited.

Mr. Doubleday did what any wise business man would do. When he was told that an unexpected visitor was asking for him, he sent his assistant, Miss Comstock, to find out what it was all about. Miss Comstock came to the library. At first she could not see anyone, and was puzzled, but then she found Escargot on top of a glass case that holds some rare manuscripts and old printed books. He was pretending to study the manuscripts with keen interest, but as a matter of fact he had climbed there with a sound business instinct. He knew that to talk upward from the floor would put him at a disadvantage.

Miss Comstock, after long experience in the publishing business, never shows surprise at anything. She welcomed Escargot with calm cordiality. He explained briefly the nature of his errand. Miss Comstock at first suggested that if they would submit the manuscript of the book when it was ready, it would have careful attention; but when Escargot pointed out the peanut wagon in the driveway, and the animals frisking about it, she felt that Mr. Doubleday would like to hear about this himself. Donny, in the hope of impressing Mr. Doubleday, had stoked up the peanut cooker to a high pressure of steam, and the little whistle was singing violently.

Miss Comstock thought it best to save time by giving Escargot a lift. They brought a little truck, such as is used to carry piles of books or paper, and on this Escargot rode into Mr. Doubleday's private office. There a tall bronzed man with a friendly face and very bright eyes was looking cheerfully at a little blackboard on which was written *Number of Books Printed Yesterday*, 28,000.

Miss Comstock introduced Escargot and placed him on a chair near Mr. Doubleday's desk. This chair has a broad green arm-piece for writing. Escargot sat there and cleared his throat.

It was now quite late in the afternoon, and Mr. Doubleday had had a secret notion of slipping off for a game of golf before dark, but you would never have known that, he was so polite. Escargot felt at ease immediately, and offered the publisher the bag of peanuts. Mr. Doubleday ate some and listened attentively.

"I have an idea for you," said Escargot.

"That's grand," said Mr. Doubleday. "That's what we need."

Escargot told about the Grape Arbor Tea Room, and about the way the stories had been told. The shrewd questions that Mr. Doubleday asked pleased him very much. He felt that they were both practical wary people and had much in common.

"It sounds like an interesting book," said Mr. Doubleday. "Is any of it written yet? Are any of you good writers?"

"We can get some help from Mr. Mistletoe," said Escargot.

"Don't you get help from anyone," said Mr. Doubleday. "You write it yourselves, in your own way. If it's written the way you tell it, it'll be all right.—I suppose you're rather a slow worker," he added doubtfully.

"Fourchette will do most of the writing," said Escargot. "She is very clever and thinks fast."

"I should like to meet her," said Mr. Doubleday. "We are not clever here, in fact we're only a bunch of farmers, but we work hard."

Escargot could see that what Mr. Doubleday said about being farmers was a joke, and he smiled pleasantly.

"I suppose you would pay us something for a book like that?" he said earnestly.

"I hope you don't expect to make a fortune out of it," said Mr. Doubleday. "Very few books do. This business is very uncertain."

Mr. Doubleday must have taken a fancy to Escargot, for they talked and talked. It grew dusk, and people began streaming out of the press on their way home, and the big windows shone with lights. The animals in the wagon were very anxious, imagining all sorts of ill fortune.

"Perhaps Escargot has got trodden on," said Donny.

"Perhaps he's got caught in one of the machines," said Fourchette.

"Perhaps Mr. Doubleday is a Frenchman and has eaten him," suggested the kittens.

And then, just when they were beginning to despair, Mr. Doubleday came out of the doorway. He was carrying Escargot on a piece of paper, which Escargot was carefully reading as he went along. The snail's eyes were stretched far out, he was reading the paper so attentively.

Fourchette's heart gave a jump, for as they got near she could see what the paper was. It was a contract, that is a promise, saying that the book would be published.

Mr. Doubleday was introduced to the others, and admired the wagon. He was impressed by the way the peanut roaster was steaming, which seemed to him to show a fine energy and enthusiasm. Dosoris kept trying to pull off his cap and hold out his hands, but Fourchette held him tight. Donny offered to give Mr. Doubleday a lift back to Oyster Bay in the wagon, but he said his car was waiting for him.

The animals were a little shy, knowing how much depended on Mr. Doubleday being pleased with them, but Escargot and the publisher were now on excellent terms.

"Get on with the book," said Mr. Doubleday, "and we'll publish it for you."

"We'll go right home and get to work," said Escargot. "Well, so long, Effendi."

They lit the red lantern and the peanut wagon rolled off toward Roslyn. They went by the back road, through the lonely fields, so that Donny could get out and have one of his barking fits.

So long!